BOOK

MW01071072

DEATH SHALL COME ON SWIFT WINGS TO HIM THAT TOUCHETH THE TOMB OF PHARAOH!

This is the curse that archaeologist Anthony Collins brings with him to Collinwood—along with the mummy of King Rehotip, whom he restores to life, dangerously insane.

Among Professor Collins' research teach is a young man Barnabas believes is really Quentin Collins in disguise. When Maggie Evans is menaced by a werewolf, he is sure of it.

Then death strikes at Collinwood. The curse seems to be taking effect. But who is the killer? The deranged King Rehotip, who is roaming at large? The disguised Quentin Collins? Or is it—as the professor suggests—Barnabas Collins himself?

Hermes Press

Published by Hermes Press, an imprint of
Herman and Geer Communications, Inc.

Daniel Herman, Publisher
Troy Musguire, Production Manager
Eileen Sabrina Herman, Managing Editor
Alissa Fisher, Graphic Design
Kandice Hartner, Senior Editor

2100 Wilmington Road
Neshannock, Pennsylvania 16105
(724) 652-0511
www.HermesPress.com; info@hermespress.com

Book design by Eileen Sabrina Herman
First printing, 2021

LCCN applied for: 10 9 8 7 6 54 3 2 1 0
ISBN 978-1-61345-231-8
ISBN Limited: 978-61345-252-3
OCR and text editing by H + G Media and Eileen Sabrina Herman
Proof reading by Eileen Sabrina Herman and Derek Littlejohn

From Dan, Louise, Sabrina, and Jacob for D'zur and Mellow

Acknowledgments: This book would not be possible without the help and encouragement of Jim Pierson and Curtis Holdings

Printed in Canada

Barnabas, Quentin and the Mummy's Curse
by Marilyn Ross

CONTENTS

CHAPTER 1

Until that morning in early December when Maggie Evans received the phone call from Professor Anthony Collins she had known little of Egypt, its sun god, Ra, or of Osiris, the god of death and resurrection, nor was she familiar with the "Books of the Dead." The coast of Maine in winter with its raw winds, ice and snow, and long dark nights was as foreign to the burning sands of Egypt as any place could be. Yet it was in Collinsport that Maggie was to be introduced to the cult of Osiris and undergo an experience stranger than any she'd known in her young life!

The winter of 1969 came early and bitter. December was marked by unusually heavy snows. After each storm the thermometer went lower, and mournful, icy winds haunted the menacing long nights. It was during those phantom nights that Collinwood was to be the scene of a drama more weird than any that had taken place there before. The ancient estate which had known the threat of the vampire, the werewolf and the zombie was now to be host to an even more macabre evil . . . an evil epitomized by a spectral, mummified hand which reached out from the grim pyramids of Egypt, half a world away, to throw its demonic shadow on the frigid snow of Collinwood in America.

Maggie had been enjoying a respite from her duties as governess to Amy and David, as Elizabeth Stoddard had decided the children should have the entire month of December as a vacation. This was chiefly because the mistress of Collinwood was taking Amy and Carolyn with her on a West Indies vacation. David, who loved skating and skiing, had elected to stay at home and enjoy these favorite winter sports. But since there was no study schedule Maggie saw little of him, except at mealtimes.

It was at the candlelit dinner table one evening that David's father, Roger Collins, informed her his cousin, Professor Anthony Collins, had retired from the staff of Boston Historical Museum and was coming back to his home in Collinsport to live and continue work on special projects.

Roger Collins refilled his wine glass as he said, "I don't believe you've met Cousin Anthony, have you?"

"No," Maggie told him. "I think I've heard Mrs. Stoddard mention him."

"Sure you have." David spoke up with all the assurance of a youngster on the edge of his teens. "He's the one who used to be always sending us cards from Europe and Africa. He went around digging up things."

Roger gave his son a reproving glance. "Your cousin Anthony Collins is a world-famous Egyptologist and you must speak of him with respect."

David frowned. "I didn't mean anything."

Maggie showed the boy a sympathetic smile. "I'm sure you didn't. But your father is right. He is an elderly gentleman and should be given due consideration."

Roger touched a napkin to his lips and then put it down. "Respect is not an attribute of the young these days. I suppose I shouldn't look for it in you."

David stood up. "I've finished dinner. May I be excused? I'd like to skate in the stable yard for awhile."

Maggie told him, "Whatever your father thinks."

"You may go out for a half-hour or so. Then come in and prepare for bed."

"Yes, sir," David said with a hint of resentment. Knowing the boy was much like his father in temperament, Maggie guessed that he would stay out an hour or longer, despite the parental orders.

She called after him. "Bundle yourself up well. It must be zero tonight."

"Yes, Miss Evans," the boy said and quickly left the dining room.

As soon as David was out of the room his father gazed at Maggie. "I fear my son is badly spoiled, Maggie."

She blushed. "He has spirit. But I think he minds as well as most boys his age. He doesn't give me too many problems."

"A firm hand, Maggie," Roger Collins advised her seriously.

"There is nothing to take the place of it. I blame Elizabeth for allowing the children too much liberty. And I can't expect to make any startling changes in David in the few weeks she's away."

"He's enjoying the winter so," Maggie said with a smile on her attractive young face.

"He's about the only one," Roger grumbled. "I can't say that I am pleased that winter has begun so early. It makes things much more difficult at the factory and I dislike the cold and snow."

"It should be especially hard on Professor Collins after all his years spent in Egypt."

"He only spent a portion of each year there," Roger said. "Much of his work was done in Boston at the museum. And as I understand it he will go on working on his own. He'll continue to make expeditions to Egypt financed by some wealthy friends who are interested in his discoveries along the Nile. And he will catalog and prepare the material he brings back in his home here. After that it will be offered to the highest bidders among the museums and private collectors."

"So he will be actually continuing his regular work though retired."

"Exactly," Roger agreed with a nod. "If all goes well both he and the syndicate proposing to back him will make money."

"Has he said when he intends to arrive?"

"I understand he is to be here tomorrow. He has the red brick house with the white trim you see as you drive into Collinwood. It's on the ocean side and close to the edge of the cliffs."

Maggie showed interest. "I've passed it every day. It's only a short walk from here."

"That's right."

With a questioning glance, she asked, "Is it true that Barnabas Collins is also returning to spend the holidays here?"

Roger looked grim. "I believe so," he said. "Elizabeth spoke to me about it before she left. I've had the old house opened and heated in case he does come. It will be the first time he's spent the holidays here for a long while."

Maggie looked pleased. *"I hope he comes. I've always found him very nice."

Roger shrugged. "I suppose he has a certain charm— that trace of a British accent, and he carries himself well." She smiled. "He's quite mod in his dress. I'm sure that caped coat comes direct from some smart London men's shop."

"No doubt. He's never been a stable type. Traveling all the time. Never marrying or settling down in any one place. It's no wonder the Collinsport people have regarded him with suspicion on his visits here."

"I say they've been much too critical of him," Maggie complained. "He's different and that's a crime in a small village like this."

"I wish he understood that," Roger said bleakly. "I've tried to advise him to dress more conventionally, give up his all-night hours and come without that wretched mute monster, Hare."

"Hare is rather formidable when you first meet him, but I'm sure he's devoted to Barnabas."

"I don't question that," the blond man said irascibly. "But I maintain that he would be still better off without him. Hare's ugly presence and his short temper have made him widely disliked. Yet Barnabas clings to the man!"

Maggie was accustomed to Roger's dinner table complaints; he often indulged in them when Elizabeth was at home. Roger was an erratic man, who occasionally drank too much. But it was embarrassing for her to sit there alone and listen to his harangue. She couldn't always agree with him and it made her feel awkward.

To change the subject, she said, "Have Professor Collins and Barnabas met?"

Roger frowned. "Once several years ago. As I remember it, Anthony didn't take to Barnabas. Nor Barnabas to him. But then they are vastly different types."

"Oh?"

"Anthony is a typical aged professor. He was still erect of figure, though sixty-five, and his hair was iron-gray when I last saw him. He has the Collins features but he's very near-sighted without his glasses so he wears them nearly all the time. This gives him a scholarly look. Of course he is precise and exact in his manner."

"Does he have a wife?"

Roger shook his head. "No. He is a bachelor like Barnabas. But a very different sort of person. He is much more retiring than Barnabas and devoted entirely to his work."

"Has the brick house been opened yet?"

"Yes. For about a week his secretary has been here getting things prepared for Anthony's arrival. She seems a very competent, pretty girl—about twenty-five I should say."

"He'll have some servants to run the house?"

"Yes. A Jack Radcliff and his wife Emma, will be living there along with a maid from the village, Bessie Miles."

"I've met her," Maggie remembered. "Last summer she worked in the Collinsport Hotel as a waitress. She's a blonde and extremely pretty."

"That's the one." It was to be expected that he'd have noticed the girl's appearance; he had a reputation of being a ladies' man.

"I must watch and see if Professor Collins arrives in the morning."

"I understand he's having two other professors here to assist him," Roger went on. "One, a retired member of the Boston Historical Museum staff like himself, is already here, a Professor James Martin. He paid me a short visit at the office. He's elderly and in rather poor health. There's another younger man from New York who has still to come."

Maggie listened with a look of interest on her attractive face. "It sounds as if the red brick house will be a busy place."

"I expect that it will. I must say any additions to the community during the long winter season will be welcome ones. Anthony often is away during the cold months on one of his expeditions. But this year he plans to work with the materials he found in the tomb of King Rehotip."

"Of course!" Maggie exclaimed. "I remember when he found the tomb. There were long articles in all the magazine sections."

"You'll probably meet Anthony when Elizabeth returns," Roger predicted. "She'll be entertaining him and his colleagues, without a doubt."

Maggie thought no more of the conversation until she was out for a walk the following morning and saw a small caravan of trucks led by a car making its way along the icy road to the red brick house of Professor Anthony Collins. She was standing on a hill near Collinwood and had an unobstructed view of the smaller house on the side road leading from the village.

The trucks came to a halt in front of the house and as she watched figures emerged from the cabs and the unloading began. Her pert face was a healthy pink from the cold air and her breath made a pattern of vapor as she drew her scarf tighter around her neck. The bright sun was reflecting against the white frozen surface of the snow, but it was still terribly cold.

Some of the crates being removed from the trucks seemed extremely heavy, as several men were required to handle them. Even then, they seemed to be straining. The unloading went on at a fairly slow pace. She saw a thin dark clad man directing the operations and guessed that this must be Professor Collins.

At last she wearied of watching the activity and began walking down to the edge of the cliffs. She made her way along the frozen surface of the snow as far as Widows' Hill. Walking gave her a respite from the cold and she was enjoying the bright winter day. Reaching the high point of the cliffs, she glanced back at Collinwood.

The sprawling old mansion with its forty rooms stood out against the snow. The winter setting made it seem more imposing than it looked in other seasons. The house was lonesome with Elizabeth and the girls away; Maggie had little to occupy her time.

She walked back to the front entrance of Collinwood and glancing down toward the brick house on the edge of the cliffs, saw that one of the trucks had already left. The other two were still being unloaded. She went on into the house.

In the hallway she paused to stare up at the oil painting of the original Barnabas Collins which had hung there for many years. The strong, sad face that gazed at her from the dark canvas with its ornate gilt frame was almost identical with that of the present-day Barnabas whom she had come to know and like. She hoped that Roger had been right and his British cousin would pay a visit to the estate.

Removing her overshoes, coat and scarf, she hung them in the hallway and went into the living room. The sun streaming in through the front windows of the elegantly appointed room made it warm and inviting. She was well inside before she noticed someone else was there already. So unexpected was the sight of the young man standing at the far end of the room gazing up at the painting of Josiah Collins above the fireplace that she gave a small gasp.

He heard her and turned to greet her with a thin smile on his pleasant face. He was in his late twenties or early thirties with light brown hair. He wore heavy sideburns and dark-rimmed glasses.

"How do you do," he said politely. He had on a fawn topcoat and carried a fur cap in his hand.

"You startled me," she told him. "I wasn't expecting to find anyone in here."

"I'm sorry," he said in a quiet voice.

"Did you come to see Mr. Roger Collins? If so he's not here. You'll find him in the village at the office of the fish packing plant."

The young man continued to smile. "As a matter of fact, I came here to see Professor Anthony Collins."

"You won't find him here," she said. "He's at the red brick house further back along the road nearer the village. I think he arrived by car just a short time ago."

He raised his eyebrows. "Then I have the wrong house? Odd! The lady who let me in didn't make that clear to me."

Maggie smiled sympathetically. "Our housekeeper, Mrs. Stamers, is rather deaf. Probably she didn't hear you clearly."

"That must have been it."

Maggie had the peculiar feeling that she'd met him at some other time but she couldn't place him. She said, "It's only a short walk from here to the professor's house. I can show you where it is. Or do you have a car?"

"No," he said. "A taxi brought me here from the village."

She looked surprised at this. "The driver should have known where to take you."

The young man smiled. "I suppose the numbers of Collinses living along this road can be confusing to the villagers. No harm done. I've been enjoying the fine paintings and rare antique furnishings of this room."

It was her turn to smile. "This is the main house on the estate. There is an older building, but most of the valuable pieces have been brought here. The Collins family takes great pride in Collinwood."

"I don't blame them," he said. "By the way, let me introduce myself. My name is Herb Price. I'm from New York. I'll be working with Professor Collins."

"You're the young professor who will help him and Professor Martin with the King Rehotip findings?"

"That's right," he agreed. "I've spent several years with various New York museums but I was anxious to get out of the city for a time. And this seemed like an interesting project and a picturesque place to spend a winter."

"You'll find it quiet," she warned him.

"I won't mind that," he said. "I am planning a book on treasures of the Nile Valley and hope to get my notes in order here."

"That sounds fascinating," Maggie said, studying the pleasant face with the thick glasses and wondering why she was haunted by the feeling of having known him before.

As they walked out to the front hall she told him who she was and what her position was in the old mansion. He listened with polite interest.

"No doubt we'll see each other again, then," he said as they stood by the front door.

"That's a certainty." She laughed. "Our social life is limited here in the winter. And Elizabeth will undoubtedly be entertaining her cousin."

"I hope you won't think archeology a boring business," Professor Price said, "because it isn't."

"I haven't thought much about it," she admitted. "But from what I've read in the newspapers you must have lots of thrilling adventures. Isn't there supposed to be some sort of curse on the King Rehotip tomb?"

He nodded. "That story was started because of the bad fortune suffered by the first expedition that attempted to open the tomb. Professor Collins was the leader of the second and successful group."

"Wasn't there some sort of inscription on the tomb?"

Herb Price looked grimly amused. "I can quote it: 'Death shall come on swift wings to him that toucheth the tomb of Pharaoh.' Does that sound sufficiently sinister?"

She gave a tiny shiver. "Indeed it does. Aren't you frightened by it?"

"Not at all," he said easily. "I know the history of the bad luck legend. It started when Lord Carter, patron of the arts and financial backer of the first group to Luxor, suddenly died of a mosquito bite a mere few days after the tomb was opened. The next year Professor Ali Behmy was shot and killed by his wife in London. And another associate of the professor's was murdered a month or so later in Cairo. The actual leader of the expedition, John Mills, committed suicide in New York last year and his father was killed in an auto accident returning from his funeral."

Maggie looked at the young man who had calmly recited this list of tragic happenings. "I'd think you'd be afraid to touch any of the King Rehotip relics!"

"Not at all," he said, "because I know many of the people on that first expedition are still alive and well. And none of Professor Collins' party has suffered any such misfortune as yet."

"As yet," she echoed as a mild warning.

He laughed. "I'm not superstitious. Archeologists can't afford to be. All those unfortunate deaths happened by chance. You have to believe that."

"I hope you are right."

He put on his fur cap. "The weather is certainly wintery up here. Is it always as cold as this?"

"It's a bad year."

"I would hope so," he said. "What about wild life? Of course you have deer and likely moose in the more northerly regions. And what about wolves?"

"I don't think so."

"I can't see why not," he argued. "You're bound to have wildcats. Wolves shouldn't be all that rare."

"I must ask." She opened the door and showed him the distant red brick house of the professor. All the trucks had gone now but there were several cars parked by it. "I think you'll find the Professor there."

Herb Price was on the steps. "I'm sure I will. Thank you for giving me so much of your time."

"I enjoyed our conversation," she said. And she had. "It's strange, but I keep having this sensation that I've seen you before."

"Really?" The eyes behind the thick glasses showed amusement. "I doubt it."

She waited by the open door a moment as he walked away from Collinwood. Then as the chill air bit into her she closed the door. She stood in the hallway, thinking. A frown crossed her pretty face. He seemed to have made himself very much at home in the mansion, as if he'd been there before and knew it well. Her reverie was interrupted as the housekeeper, Mrs. Stamers, showed herself on the stairs.

Maggie went over to meet the elderly deaf woman as she reached the foot of the stairs. "Did you recognize that young man you let in here a little while ago?"

Mrs. Stamers stared at her with a blank look on her round face. "What young man?"

She regarded the stout woman with astonishment. "The young man you showed into the living room."

"But I didn't show anyone in there," the old woman protested. "I've been working upstairs for at least an hour." She looked worried and glanced towards the double doors leading to the big living room. "Is he in there now?"

"No. But he was here. He left just a few minutes ago. And he said that you let him in."

"Then he was lying, miss," the stout woman said indignantly. "Would he be some kind of thief?"

Maggie shook her head. "No. He identified himself. He's here to work with Professor Anthony Collins at the red brick house."

"Oh, that one."

She frowned. "But why did he come here? And why did he just walk in and then pretend you'd let him in?"

"Sounds like he wasn't up to any good!"

"I won't judge him until I'm more sure of my facts," Maggie said.

"That front door should be kept locked," Mrs. Stamers worried. "But it isn't."

Maggie could see that the old woman was deeply concerned. She was, as well, but there seemed no point in bothering Mrs. Stamers more. So she said, "I'm sure it was just a misunderstanding. Please don't think about it anymore."

Mrs. Stamers looked less than satisfied. "I won't be able to get it off my mind," she fretted. "I feel doubly responsible with Mrs. Stoddard away."

"We all do," Maggie said. "But this is nothing you should be upset about."

Mrs. Stamers, finally placated, walked back to the kitchen. As she vanished into the shadows of the corridor Maggie watched her. It was likely the young man had tried to get the deaf woman's attention and when that hadn't been possible he'd opened the door and let himself in. A brazen thing to do, but considering the cold and the fact he had no criminal intentions, something she could understand.

Still the incident stayed in her mind. Later in the afternoon David came in, chapped and breathless from his exertions in the snow. He was full of excitement about the activity at the red brick house. "There must have been a ton of stuff they carried in. Some of the boxes were about the shape and size of coffins. Do you suppose they were dead people the professor brought back from Egypt with him?"

"They could be mummies," she admitted. "There is usually more than one in all the tombs."

"Gosh!" David said, eyes glowing. "Do you suppose they'd let me look at them?"

"Later on." She smiled. "I'm sure they'll place at least some of their finds on public view."

"I'll want to be there," David promised as he went upstairs to wash for dinner.

When Roger returned home he confirmed that Anthony Collins had arrived. "He's here to remain for a couple of months, perhaps three or four. As long as it takes to catalog the King Rehotip collection."

"An odd thing happened here this morning," she told Roger. And she went on to explain how she'd found Professor Herb Price in the living room and the fact he'd lied about how he'd gotten into the house.

Roger looked unhappy. "Why should he do that?"

"I've tried to decide and haven't come up with any truly satisfactory answers," she said. "The best I've managed is that Mrs. Stamers didn't hear him at the door and he became tired of standing in the cold. So he just walked in. When I discovered him he was too embarrassed to admit what he'd done."

"Possibly," Roger said. "But I can't see why he came to Collinwood in the first place. The taxi driver would have known Anthony Collins was at the red brick house."

"I worried about that too," she agreed. "But he appeared very mild and pleasant. And nothing was touched. So he must be all right. The one other odd thing is that he seemed familiar to me."

"Oh?" Roger waited for her to enlarge on this.

She made a tiny futile gesture. "I could be wrong but I think I may have seen him somewhere before. But he wasn't wearing glasses as he is now. Glasses make quite a difference in people."

"Did you mention this to him?"

"I did but he brushed it off."

Roger looked grim. "He sounds like a pretty smooth customer. The first chance I get I'll question Anthony about him."

"That wouldn't do any harm."

Later that evening, after David had gone to bed and Roger had retired to his study to take care of some paper work he'd brought home from the plant, Maggie sat alone in the living room reading. She'd turned on only one tri-lamp and was seated in the otherwise dark room directly under its light.

The memory of the young man who'd appeared so unexpectedly at the house that morning still haunted her. And as a sudden wintery gust rattled the shutters of the ancient mansion she felt a chill of fear go through her. And then from a long distance away there came a weird, wolflike howling.

She went rigid with fear and jumped up from her chair with frightened eyes. Recalling Professor Price's casual mention of possible wolves, she went across to the window and drew back a drape to stare out into the darkness. Frost on the pane hindered her view and she saw nothing. But once again there came the eerie howling. Then it was silent. Silent, except for an occasional moaning of the night wind.

CHAPTER 2

Shortly after breakfast the following morning a lazy snowstorm began. Maggie turned on the television for the weather report and there was a warning that the storm might become a heavy one before nightfall. Roger Collins had gone to the fishing plant in the village and David was sulking before the living room window, staring gloomily out at the snow.

Maggie joined him and put a hand on his shoulder. "What's wrong?" she asked with a smile.

David frowned. "I haven't got anything to do."

"You'll have plenty of fun when the storm ends," she said. "And you'll be able to help clean out the walks as well."

"I wanted to skate," he complained.

She gave him a teasing look. "You should have gone with your aunt and the girls. You'd be swimming right now."

David looked up at her. "I don't want to swim. I want to skate."

"Wait until the storm ends."

He gave her a questioning look. "Did you hear that wild animal howl last night?"

"Yes, I did."

"Boy, it sure sounded creepy," David said with a shiver. "I wouldn't want to meet up with whatever it was."

"You're lucky to be in a nice warm house."

"What do you suppose it was?"

"I couldn't guess," she said, not caring to admit she'd been scared by the howling.

"I never heard anything like it before," David said.

"Why don't you go upstairs and work on one of the jigsaw puzzles?" she suggested.

David thrust his hands in his pockets and ambled off in a boyish sulky fashion. "Guess I will," he said. And then from part way up the stairs. "But there's no fun in that. I wish Amy was back."

Maggie smiled sadly to herself. She too wished the others were home. Collinwood seemed strangely silent and empty without them. She thought Roger felt the same way. She continued to stand by the window, for a few minutes longer watching the huge snowflakes waft lazily down. Then the phone rang.

She went to the extension in the front hall and picked up the receiver. At once a reedy male voice asked, "May I speak with Miss Maggie Evans?"

"This is she."

"Ah, Miss Evans." The reedy voice sounded pleased. "I'm happy to have been able to contact you so easily. This is Professor Anthony Collins speaking. You've probably heard of me. I own the red brick house facing the sea."

"Yes, I know about you and your work, Professor Collins," she said politely.

"Of course you do," the old man's voice agreed. "Professor Price was at Collinwood through error yesterday. You met him then."

"I did."

"It was very kind of you to straighten him out and send him to us," the professor went on. "My reason for calling you is that we need additional help here. My secretary is very busy. I want a young woman to assist me and also to occasionally help her with the secretarial work. I phoned my cousin, Roger, and suggested you might be available for a few weeks until his sister returns."

Maggie was surprised. "I'm actually supposed to be working for Mrs. Stoddard in her absence."

"I realize that," the professor said. "But Roger has offered to be responsible for having you hire out to me for a few weeks. I'm sure you'd find the work interesting and I do need someone badly."

Maggie hesitated. It was boring being alone in the old mansion with David and the few servants all day. But would David be lost without her and would Elizabeth be angry at her taking this other position, even on a temporary basis?

She said, "I'll think it over."

"Why not walk down and see me this morning?" the elderly professor suggested. "If you feel you would enjoy the work you can accept my offer. We'll have no trouble about terms."

"It's storming," she said. "But if it doesn't get worse I'll go over and discuss it with you."

"Excellent," Professor Collins said. "I'll be looking for you." And the phone clicked at the other end of the line.

Maggie put the receiver down and stood there in the gray light of the hallway with a perplexed look on her pretty face. After a moment she decided to call Roger Collins at the plant.

It took a few minutes to get him to the phone. When he answered, she told him about the professor's call, ending with, "I didn't want to make any promises until I'd discussed it with you."

"I understand," Roger said. "I think it would be a good idea to give Anthony some help. It's bound to be interesting, and you're not needed at Collinwood."

"What about David?"

"He'll be safe enough in Mrs. Stamers' care," his father said. "And any day it is storming he can come down to the plant with me. I can always find him some small job to keep him busy."

"Professor Collins asked me to see him this morning."

"Then go and talk with him," Roger advised. "And if the old man is serious about hiring you, by all means take the job. I'll make it all right with Elizabeth."

So the question was settled. Maggie let Mrs. Stamers know she was going out and told her to get David's lunch at the proper time. Then she put on her winter clothing and went out into the storm. The snowfall had brought warmer air and it was actually pleasant walking amid the lazy snowflakes, though she did notice that the storm was gradually getting heavier.

She was not able to get a clear view of the ocean through the curtain of falling snow. It was a lot like when the fog came in. Not much snow had collected on the ground yet, but it would as the day went on. Soon she saw the outline of the red brick house ahead of her. And as she drew near it she realized it was a good deal larger than she'd imagined from seeing it at a distance.

An open gate and a fairly long driveway led to the house, which was perched almost on the edge of the cliff. To the side of the big house there was a parking area with several cars and a station wagon in it. Smoke came out of the chimney in a black flow but did not rise high.

The three steps before the entrance door were of the same brick as the body of the house, with an iron railing on either side of them. She mounted the steps and lifted the brass door knocker. In a few minutes the door was opened by a dark-haired, stunning girl in her late twenties. She had large green eyes and a ready smile. Yet there was an air of brisk authority about her that suggested she might have a dominating personality. She was wearing a light gray smock over a dark wool minidress.

Maggie introduced herself and said, "I think Professor Collins is expecting me."

"You're quite right," the other girl said crisply. "Please come in. I'm Harriet Fennel, the professor's secretary. We're having a dreadful time getting things straightened out here."

As she entered the living room Maggie noted that this was true. Large packing cases were set down amid the furniture, some of which still had ghostly white throws over it.

She smiled at the dark girl. "You've only been here less than a day."

Harriet Fennel gestured at the packing cases with despair. "It's like this everywhere except in the upstairs bedrooms and the kitchen. We have just too much material to go over. In the museums we were always short of storage space. But never anything like this."

"I'm not sure that I can be of any help," Maggie faltered.

"Any extra hands that are willing can be of assistance in a situation like this," Harriet Fennel declared. "I'll get Professor Collins. He's busy in the cellar with his associates. We have our main workshop in the cellar." And with that the attractive brunette left the living room.

Maggie stood there waiting. Her eyes wandered from one wooden packing case to another. There were none of the coffin-shaped ones in the room but there were some large ones, square-shaped, and many small flat boxes. She saw black lettering which indicated they had been shipped from Cairo and noted each box was numbered. She tried to picture the precious items that might be in them.

The treasures of King Rehotip had been termed fabulous in all the newspaper stories she had read. When a king died, the chambers of his sepulcher were filled with rich furniture, beds, couches, and chairs inlaid with ivory and gold and chests of clothing. There would also be weapons, jewelry, pottery along with food and wine to serve his every need in the hereafter.

She heard footsteps approaching and looked up to see a tall, bony man with iron-gray hair and the strong features characteristic of the Collins family. But he wore rimless glasses which gave prominence to his fanatical blue eyes. He was also wearing a gray smock over a dark suit and he offered a thin, hairy hand in greeting.

"Miss Evans," he said, showing a smile and speaking in his excited, reedy voice. "How kind of you to come."

"I wanted to find out what sort of work I'd have to do."

He ran a hand over his bushy iron-gray hair and waved to the array of wooden boxes cluttering the room with the other. "As you can see, we're swamped with material from the tomb of King Rehotip. The sooner I can open the various cases, examine and value the contents for catalog purposes, the sooner I will be able to cope with the confusion here."

"I know nothing of this kind of work," she warned him.

"No need," he said. "I'll pay you the same salary you've been getting at Collinwood and you'll act as my personal assistant, copying down what I dictate as I open the cases. And as soon as Elizabeth returns I'll free you to go back to your regular work."

"It sounds fair enough," she agreed. "You must have brought back some wonderful things."

"All that the Egyptian government would allow," Anthony Collins said with a sudden bleak look. "They frequently seem to regard expeditions like mine as grave-robbing forays rather than attempts to discover, restore and perpetuate the history of their civilization and that of all mankind. As you know the first expedition failed miserably. All they discovered was an empty tomb which had been vandalized over the years!"

"And didn't many of them suffer from what the newspapers called the Curse of Osiris?"

Anthony Collins looked disgusted. "Cheap sensationalism. I've been an Egyptologist most of my life and opened many tombs. Neither myself nor any of my associates have experienced ill effects from our work."

"But in the case of King Rehotip the curse was something special," she said. "Wasn't it clearly carved over the entrance to the tomb?"

"It was," Anthony Collins agreed. "But that curse had nothing to do with the many sudden deaths among the members of the first expedition. I can only point out that we succeeded where the others failed and we haven't suffered any ill from it."

She smiled. "At least not yet."

The old professor studied her suspiciously with those pale blue eyes behind his glasses. "You're not superstitious, I hope?"

"Not really."

"Good," he said. "For I must warn you, we have the embalmed dead bodies of King Rehotip and several of his court below in the cellar. Within a few days I shall be opening the sarcophagus containing the body of Rehotip. It is an occasion I look forward to. For the first time in thousands of years the body of that warrior monarch will be exposed to the light. And if I'm not mistaken you'll see a perfect example of the ancient art of embalming as practiced by the Egyptians."

"It sounds a little morbid."

"Not at all," he protested. "I was extremely fortunate to find all these things hidden in a tomb behind the main tomb that had been vandalized. One night a workman led me to the lonely tomb, hollowed in a hillside, and there I was privileged to see something which few men have ever seen. He shone his flashlight through a hole in the rear wall of the tomb and I saw a scene from thousands of years ago. A collection of small, painted wood models so lifelike I might have been witnessing a living drama. There were models of ships with their crews to provide the king with passage along the Nile. And hidden beneath the display of models was the king's gilded coffin. And near the coffin were treasures such as silver mirrors, toilet vases with perfumed ointments and even small copper razors. There was a girdle made of hollow golden shells in the form of lion heads and joined by rows of amethyst beads, and many other precious items, including some priceless jeweled scarabs which were confiscated by the Egyptian officials."

As the professor concluded his account on this mournful note he looked dejected. She could see that he was obsessed by his interest in his work, that his pale blue eyes with their strange brightness marked him as a fanatic. For just a moment she wondered if she really wanted to work for this odd man.

Then Professor Price appeared in the doorway of the living room. The brown-haired young man had also donned a gray smock and he looked genuinely pleased to see her.

"I hear you've decided to join us grave-diggers," was his first comment as he came over to her and the professor.

She smiled. "I haven't definitely made up my mind."

"You should. We're doing an important work and we badly need help."

Professor Collins nodded vigorously. "Try and persuade her, Price. I believe she is worried about the King Rehotip curse."

Herb smiled. "None of the rest of us are worried."

"I've told her it's a myth created by the sensation-hungry press," the old man grumbled.

Maggie smiled at them both. "I'll take your word for it. When do you want me to begin work?"

"This very minute," Professor Collins said. "Is there any reason why you can't remain here for the balance of the day?"

She hesitated. "Not really. Although the storm may get worse by the time it's dark."

"Don't worry," the young professor told her. "I'll see you safely back to Collinwood."

Anthony Collins beamed. "You see? There is no problem!"

"I don't want to cause needless bother."

"No bother," Herb Price said. "I'll enjoy walking you back there."

Anthony Collins interjected, "I think it might be a good idea for you to plan to live in here while you are working with us. Our hours are by no means nine to five. And this would be much more practical."

"I'd have to gather some things together," Maggie said. "I could do that tonight."

"Fine," the old man said. "I deeply appreciate Roger allowing you to work for me. Now I'll take you downstairs and find a smock for you.

Also I'd like to introduce you to the others."

Herb Price gave her a smile of encouragement as she followed Anthony Collins out of the room. The old man led her to a dark hallway and a door at the end of it which opened on a flight of rickety wooden steps. With the venerable professor leading the way she slowly made her way down to the cellar level.

The cellar was divided into a number of rooms. The first one they entered was primitively lighted by a bare bulb hanging from a ceiling cord, giving off a yellowish murky glow. The floor was of hard earth and the partitions were of rough boards with small spaces between them.

This first room was filled with wooden cases. The old man weaved his way through them to take her to the next room. It was like the first except that there was a table with some small boxes of filing cards and scattered papers on it. An old man sat at the table writing something. He looked up with a slightly startled expression as they entered. He was frail and appeared to be eighty or more.

Anthony Collins came close to the old man and spoke loudly in his ear. "This is Miss Maggie Evans, my new assistant." And turning to her, he continued, "Professor James Martin, my senior colleague and a true credit to our profession."

The old man's thin, yellowish face showed a slight smile. His eyes were sunken and his head bald. With his hollow cheeks and shiny false teeth he seemed more like a Death's head than a human being.

"Happy to meet you, Miss Evans." When he spoke he wheezed badly.

"My pleasure, Professor Martin."

Anthony Collins let her waste no time with the old man but quickly led her into a third room where Harriet Fennel was busily cleaning a small stone figure of a cat which she'd taken from one of the open cases. This room also had a table with provision for cataloging. The dark girl paused in her work to greet Maggie with a nod. "So you have decided to join us?"

"Yes," Maggie told her. "The professor is difficult to argue with."

"I could have warned you of that."

Professor Collins chuckled. "Only in a good cause. We'll go on to the fourth and last of our work rooms." This proved to be the biggest of all. There was a regular desk and a swivel chair in one corner of it; the desktop was a confusion of papers. Still only one rather dim light bulb served this large room and didn't do much more than disperse the shadows. The floor was earthen and although there was an old-fashioned hot water radiator in each of the cellar rooms, Maggie felt they were damp and cold. No doubt because of the earthen floors. She also noticed with a tiny feeling of fear that it was in this room the several coffins were spaced neatly along one wall.

Anthony Collins went over to a rack and brought her a gray

smock similar to the ones worn by the others. With a smile on his lined face, he said, "Put that on and we'll begin."

Maggie felt more comfortable in the smock. With notebook and pencil in hand she followed the professor while he went about opening case after case. She wrote down his comments on each item and would type this material on filing cards later. So in the dank, murky atmosphere of the cellars on that stormy day she began to learn something about Egyptology.

She heard from the old professor's lips of the growth of the cult of the dead in ancient Egypt. And she was shown shabtis, which represented the dead in miniature, not as they appeared in Ufe, but as a wrapped mummy. Osiris and his wife Isis played an important part in the offering formulas with which these little mummiform figures were inscribed. Their main function was to provide an alternate haven for the spirit in the event the actual mummy were by some chance destroyed. In time the tiny mummified figures took on the role of magical servant. And they replaced the representations of real servants formerly used in such tombs. It was a realm of the dead of which she was learning, a world devoted entirely to the tomb and the embalmer's hand.

If she'd had any doubts of Anthony Collins being a fanatic before they were settled by the time the day ended. He kept her in the dank, dusty atmosphere of the poorly lighted room until it was six o'clock. And he only let her go then with some misgivings because Herb Price came to tell her he was ready to walk her back to Collinwood.

Anthony Coffins told her in leaving, "Be prepared to remain here beginning tomorrow."

As the young professor escorted her up the rickety wooden stairs he told her, "Be prepared for a surprise. The storm is really heavy now."

When she reached the upstairs and looked out the window she saw that he was right. Even in the darkness she could see the snow beating down blindingly.

Moving to the front door to put on her coat and overshoes she met Harriet Fennel. The dark girl gave her an appraising look. "How did you enjoy your first taste of Egyptology?"

Maggie was fastening her overshoes. She looked up at the other girl with a smile. "It has a lot to do with the grave."

"Wait until you see some of those wizened mummies," Harriet said with cold amusement.

Professor Price came into the room with his outdoor clothing on. "I'm ready. What about you?"

She was tying a kerchief around her hair. "I can find my way all right. There's no need for you to come with me."

"I wouldn't think of allowing you to walk back alone on this stormy night."

Harriet was watching them with a disdainful expression. And she told Herb Price, "I didn't know you had taken on extra duties."

He smiled. "For tonight anyway," he said. "Maggie begins living in tomorrow."

The dark girl lifted her eyebrows as if this wasn't exactly pleasing news. "Oh? Then you're not discouraged?" she asked Maggie.

"Not yet," Maggie said, enjoying what she guessed might be a kind of jealousy on the dark girl's part. Harriet had apparently decided that the young professor was her property. She hadn't counted on Maggie for competition.

"Let's go," Herb said happily and opened the front door. A gust of wind burst in, bringing snow with it. Maggie gave a tiny, excited laugh and bracing herself, stepped out into the stormy darkness. Herb closed the door after them and grasped her by the arm. Then they began walking through the fairly deep snow with heads bowed against the storm.

"It almost takes your breath," she gasped.

"Keep your head down," he advised. "It's easier that way and you don't get so blinded." He had a large flashlight in his free hand but they couldn't see any distance even in its strong beam.

She gave another small troubled laugh. "I hope we know which way we're going."

"We'll manage," he promised. "What did you make of it all?"

Head still bent down, she said, "It's kind of creepy. All those things that were buried so long with the dead. And those coffins with the bodies in them."

"You'll get so you don't mind them," he promised. "What did you think of Professor Martin?"

"A strange old man."

"He's very old and a victim of recurring malaria. Every so often he has a brief blackout. Usually loses a half-day when he is hit by one of those spells. But he has wonderful ambition."

"You can tell that."

"Harriet is capable and devoted to Professor Collins but she's a bitter, frustrated young woman," Herb Price said. "I'd try to keep her a friend. I'd say she could make a bad enemy."

She gave him a sidelong glance, her head still bowed against the storm. "I think she has an eye on you. She certainly seems to resent me."

"I wouldn't let it worry you."

"It's strange," she told him. "But you really do remind me of someone. I can't be sure who. But I have the conviction we've met before."

"I hardly think so."

She raised her eyes to see if she could catch a glimpse of Collinwood ahead, but she could see only the blinding snow. It made her feel dizzy. "The storm is really coming down now."

"Yes," Herb Price said, his voice suddenly taking on an odd

gasping quality.

She glanced at him in alarm, thinking the storm might have been too much for him. His face looked white and drawn. "Is anything wrong?" she asked worriedly.

Keeping his head bowed slightly, he said, "No. I suddenly don't feel too well. I may have to go back." His pace was slacking.

Maggie halted and gave him a frightened look. "You really seem ill. I'd better help you. Or perhaps we should go on to Collinwood. We may be near there."

"No," he said, staring at her with anguish in his eyes. "I have some medicine back at the house."

Before she could answer, there came a mournful howling like the wolf call she'd heard the night before. It seemed very near. She gave him a terrified look. "What can that mean?"

The young professor was so obviously in torment now, his face distorted with pain, she feared he might collapse at once. "Here!" he said thrusting the flashlight into her hand. "Take that and keep on walking straight ahead. You'll be all right!" And with that he turned to run off into the storm. In a moment she'd lost sight of him.

She stood there in the driving storm, too filled with terror to move. "Herb!" she cried. "Herb Price!" But only the mocking wind answered her.

In near panic she began stumbling on ahead. She wasn't certain she was taking the right direction. But she could only pray that she was. On a night such as this the falling snow muted every sound, including the roar of the waves on the beach before Collinwood. It would be terribly easy to reach the edge of the cliffs and stumble to her death on this stormy night.

Her own breath was coming in painful gasps now as she raced on against the storm in panic. The deep snow underfoot made every step seem as if she wore leaden shoes. And again from not far away came the eerie wolf call, a howling that cut through the silencing barrier of the snowfall and set her nerves on edge!

What did those frightening wolf calls mean and what had happened to Herb Price? She worried that he might not safely make it back to the red brick house. And for that matter, had she missed her own destination?

She was nearly convinced that she was headed in the wrong direction when all at once the black hulk and yellow window lights of Collinwood loomed through the storm. With a deep sigh of relief she forced herself onward.

And then without warning a dark figure suddenly blocked her way. She halted and threw the beam of the flashlight on the figure to discover the caped coat and gaunt, noble face of Barnabas Collins!

CHAPTER 3

"Barnabas!" she cried happily, and ran forward into his arms.

For a moment Barnabas held her close to him—long enough to tell from her pounding heart that she'd been through an ordeal. Then he released her a little to ask, "What are you doing out on such a night?"

She smiled. "It's a long story. But I might ask you the same question?"

His gaunt face showed a grimly amused look. The snowflakes fell on his brownish-black hair and melted almost instantly. He said, "I have just arrived for a visit. I was on my way from the old house to Collinwood to pay my respects to Roger."

"You managed to get here in this storm?" she marveled.

"It was no problem," he said in his usual casual fashion. Then, an arm around her, he began leading her toward the front entrance of Collinwood. They reached the steps in a few minutes and Barnabas touched the doorbell.

Stout Mrs. Stamers opened the door to them and gave a shocked cry on seeing Maggie. "Miss Evans, we were so worried about you out on this night!" And then noting Barnabas, she added, "How are you, Mr. Barnabas?"

Barnabas smiled and shook the snow from his caped coat as they stood in the hallway. "We joined our resources and had no trouble getting here."

Mrs. Stamers was hovering over Maggie like a mother hen, helping her off with her coat and the drenched kerchief. Then she assisted her with her overshoes. "You poor dear!" she worried. "You could wind up with pneumonia!"

Roger came out of the study as the old woman hurried off. The blond middle-aged man surveyed them both with some wonder. "I hardly expected to see you two together tonight."

Maggie said, "I was lost in the storm. Barnabas found me."

Roger frowned. "I knew Anthony had kept you at his place too long. He should have known better on a night like this."

"I didn't realize the time."

Roger looked angry. "At least one of them could have come home with you."

She said, "The young professor, Herb Price, did start out with me. But along the way he was overtaken by some strange sort of spell and he left me."

"Anthony has collected a queer lot of people around him," was Roger's grim opinion. "Was that the same young man who appeared here without any warning or permission yesterday? The one you felt you'd seen before?"

"Yes."

"I must take this up with Anthony." Then he turned to Barnabas. "And so you are back, Barnabas. Did you find everything in order in the old house? I had the doors unlocked and some fires put on."

"It's comfortable as usual," Barnabas said with a melancholy smile. "My thanks for your kindness to me."

The blond man looked bleak. "Elizabeth would want to do it and since she's away on holiday I try to carry out what I believe would be her wishes."

"You've done well."

"That depends on the point of view from which you look at it. Have you brought Hare with you again?"

"I wouldn't consider traveling without him," Barnabas assured him. "Hare is a most reliable fellow."

"An undesirable fellow!" Roger said with some anger.

"That would be more like it. I can't understand why you bring him back year after year, knowing the villagers fear and dislike him."

"They don't understand him," Barnabas protested.

"And some of their unhappiness and suspicion extends even to you," Roger warned him. "If he creates any fuss during your visit here this time I'll make you dismiss him!"

Barnabas seemed perturbed. "I'll vouch for the man."

Roger made an impatient gesture. "We've spent enough time

and energy arguing about that ruffian. Now come into the living room and warm yourselves by the fireplace." They followed him into the big living room and she took an easy chair before the fireplace with Barnabas standing near the chair but back from the fire. She remembered he always seemed able to stand any amount of cold. Often the old house would be unheated and yet he'd never complain. His hands and lips were also cold to the touch.

Roger stationed himself with his back towards the blazing log fire as he faced her and Barnabas. He told her, "David has had his dinner and is up in his room watching television. I'll see Mrs. Stamers has our dinners ready in a few minutes."

Barnabas said, "I have already had food."

Roger paused to stare at him oddly. "I forgot. You have your own special diet."

"Yes," the gaunt-faced man said evenly. "And I don't propose to change it."

"I understand that," Roger said, going out and leaving them alone.

Barnabas stared down at her in the easy chair and she was amazed to observe how little he'd changed since they'd last met. Indeed, he hadn't aged at all.

The deep-set eyes were fixed on her as he asked, "What is all this about you being at the red brick house and Cousin Anthony having moved back there?"

She explained, ending, "So he has set up a kind of museum in his own house. Needing extra help to sort out the treasures of King Rehotip, he called on me. Roger gave me permission to go there."

Barnabas' gaunt, handsome face darkened. "Roger made a mistake in allowing that."

She stared up at him earnestly. "Do you really think so?"

Barnabas nodded. "Yes. You must have read those stories about the discovery of Rehotip's tomb and the curse associated with it."

"Professor Collins claims that is all nonsense."

"Anthony always did have strange ideas. He has been associated with Egyptology so long he's lost respect for what such a curse can mean."

"I mentioned it to him and all those deaths of the members of the first expedition," she said. "And he insisted they were due to coincidence."

Barnabas looked grim. "What will he say when the curse begins to strike him and those working with him?"

Her eyes widened with fear. "Do you think that will happen?"

"There's a strong chance of it."

Maggie considered. "That young professor doesn't seem well.

He had a strange seizure during the storm tonight. As he raced off into the snow I heard a wolf howl."

"Did you?" he commented quietly. "That is strange indeed. I have never known any wolves to show themselves in this part of New England."

"I've never thought about it before," Maggie went on. "But when he was here yesterday he spoke of wolves. And it was after that I began to hear them in the night."

His eyes met hers. "Where did this Professor Herb Price come from?"

"New York, I believe," she said. "As I understand it Anthony advertised for an assistant and he answered the advertisement."

"Then my cousin probably knows little about him. I have an idea he is so anxious for help with this project he'll take on anyone."

"Don't you consider Anthony Collins competent?"

"Competent enough," Barnabas said. "But in this case fanatically reckless. He is carrying on a study of the Rehotip treasures without any regard for a curse that I, for one, believe to have strong supernatural power. And it seems to me the fate of so many of the others who've defiled the tomb has proven this!"

"What's this talk about defiling tombs?" Roger Collins demanded as he came back into the room.

"I question this project of Anthony's" Barnabas told him. "And I think you made a mistake in allowing Maggie to work for him."

Roger's face darkened. "Are you suggesting I'm not taking proper care of this young woman?"

"I don't think you gave it sufficient thought."

"You and Anthony have never gotten along," Roger reminded him.

Barnabas shrugged. "That has no bearing on this."

"Of course it has," Roger argued. "You're prejudiced against our cousin. That's why you want to prevent Maggie from working for him."

"I'm thinking more of the curse than anything else. Do you have any idea how death stalked the other expedition that attempted to raid that tomb? I don't want to see Maggie in any danger. Anthony has a right to jeopardize his own life if he likes, but I don't think he should drag others into the shadow of the curse of Osiris."

Roger looked nasty. "I'm not up on those fancy names like you, Barnabas, but I'll match my good sense against yours any day. Especially when you hire someone like Hare!"

Maggie felt it was time to intervene. She gave them both a mild smile. "Please don't quarrel on my account," she begged them. "I've really made my own decision in the matter. I plan to work with Professor Collins until Elizabeth returns. I think it will be a rewarding experience."

Barnabas said, "You are aware of the hazards?"

"I can't see that they are great," she told him. "After all, I'll be working almost within sight of Collinwood. If I find things are not what I expected I can leave there at any time."

"Of course you can," Roger said, in a better humor. "Now I suggest we have our dinner. Barnabas, why don't you join us at the table and have a sherry while we eat?"

So the argument did not develop into a quarrel. In the soft candlelight of the dining room they all relaxed. Occasionally they were reminded of the storm outside by the harsh beating of snow against the windows like the scraping of ghostly fingers. Barnabas sat with a glass of sherry before him and several times touched it to his lips but she noticed that he never seemed to actually drink much of it.

After dinner they went back to the living room again. This time the conversation turned to the history of Collinwood. And Maggie listened with rapt attention to tales she had known before and heard new ones with amazement that the ancient mansion had been the scene of so many fantastic happenings. Roger spoke of the hidden room that had once played a major role in the lives of the family. And Barnabas talked of the Phantom Mariner and the legend of Widows' Hill. He also talked of his experiences in the isolated swamp beyond the cemetery. Suitable conversation for this stormy night as they sat before the blazing fireplace.

Then it was time to retire. Roger said goodnight and went upstairs, leaving Maggie to see Barnabas to the door. As soon as she and Barnabas were alone they relaxed a good deal. On his last visit there had been more than a hint of romance between them, and since she did not yet understand why Barnabas felt there was no future for them she still had hopes the flame might be renewed. They stood in the shadowed hallway together, the dark handsome man in the caped coat and the petite, lovely girl, with the gentle smiles of those who had been lovers on their faces. Smiles of understanding and tolerance.

She listened to the storm with concern. "I don't like to think of you trudging back to the old house on a night like this."

Barnabas laughed lightly. "I shall find it an adventure. I may even walk about in the storm for the pure pleasure of it for a while." He gave her a teasing glance. "Maybe I'll encounter that wolf you've been hearing?"

"Oh, no!" she protested. "Go straight home. In any case I don't think it can be a wolf. It's probably some unfortunate stray dog."

"Perhaps," he said dryly. "Are you determined to go to the red brick house to live and work for a few weeks?"

"Yes. But you can visit me there."

"Anthony and I do not get along too well."

Maggie smiled ruefully. "But you must try!"

"I shall," he promised. "Yet I won't deny I still wish you wouldn't expose yourself to that ancient curse."

"I'm sure there's nothing to fear."

The gaunt, handsome face of Barnabas showed melancholy amusement. "How reckless you innocents are." He sighed. "I suppose we must try and protect you from your own bad judgment."

She laughed. "Now you're being the wise older man. I like you in a more romantic mood."

With a twinkle in his deep-set eyes, Barnabas took her in his arms for a lasting kiss. She surrendered completely to those cold lips to which she'd become accustomed. They were no indicators of the warmth and charm of this solitary and lonely man.

He let her go, saying, "Now I must be on my way." His hand on the doorknob, he lingered to add, "Incidentally, I'd be careful in my friendship with that Professor Price if I were you. When the time comes I'll meet him and perhaps be able to offer you some interesting judgment about him."

She frowned. "Do you mean he's not trustworthy?"

"I'm reserving my opinion until we meet," Barnabas told her. "Meanwhile, take care." And with that rather puzzling warning he stepped out into the stormy darkness.

With the door nearly closed, she watched until he had vanished in the driving snow storm. Then with a small sigh she shut the door and switched off the hall light. In spite of all her good intentions she had done no packing in preparation for moving to the red brick house in the morning. Well, she could pack quickly in the morning. There was bound to be a delay in leaving since the road would have to be plowed after this heavy snow ontop of the previous ones. With this comforting thought she prepared for bed.

Her rest was disturbed by dreams in which a grim-faced Egyptian king burst out of his solid gold coffin to stalk her with his symbols of authority in his hands. He advanced on her in a cavernous place of shadows holding his crook and flail over her in a threatening fashion. She screamed and pleaded for mercy as he began to whip her with the flail. Then she blacked out and this nightmare was followed by another one in which a mummified figure emerged from a stone sarcophagus to come after her. So all through the night!

When she awoke the next morning the sun was shining. And after she'd showered and was dressed she heard the roar of the snow plow as it came up the road towards Collinwood. The plow was owned by the fish packing plant and as soon as the main road was opened by the highway plow it was sent to Collinwood to clear away the snow.

She guessed that by the time she'd had breakfast and packed Roger would be able to drive her to the red brick house on his way to the plant. This proved to be correct. David was at the door to see her leave and looking none too happy about it.

"I won't have any fun here at all now you're going!" the boy lamented.

"Of course you will," she said. "The skiing should be great. And you'll be able to come and visit me and see all those strange things the professor has brought back from Egypt."

"Can I?" David asked, his face brightening.

Later, as Roger drove her along the freshly plowed road to the professor's house, he frowned and said, "You're sure this is what you want to do? You don't feel you're being forced into it?"

She gave him a smiling side glance. "Of course not. I thought you were in favor of my taking the extra job."

"I am," he said at once. "But Elizabeth would never forgive me if anything happened to you. And Barnabas worried me a little last night with all that talk about a curse."

"You mustn't think about it," she said. "I'm looking forward to the experience."

Roger halted the car at the entrance to the red brick house and took her bags to the door. This time it was the redhaired maid, Bessie Miles, who let her in, saying warmly, "Do come in. Your room is ready. Jack Radcliff will bring up your bags in a minute."

Her room was on the second floor at one end of the house with a window from which she could see Collinwood high on a distant hill. Her other window faced the ocean. The room was furnished in Colonial style, a color scheme of white and blue.

Bessie smiled at her. "I think you'll like it. I have my room in the attic just above this. It's smaller but has the same view and it is quiet."

Maggie nodded as she took in the pleasant room. "It's very nice," she said. "I remember you from the hotel last summer."

Bessie looked pleased. "I was a waitress."

"I don't suppose there's enough business in the winter time to keep a full staff employed."

"That's it," the girl agreed. "I was lucky to get this job even though it's a way from the village. But otherwise I'd have had to go to Bangor or Portland for work."

At this point Jack Radcliff came puffing into the room with

Maggie's luggage. He was a short, bandy-legged man with a rather stupid weathered face and a shock of sandy hair. He left the bags and went out, merely grunting in answer to Maggie's thanks.

Bessie's green eyes sparkled with laughter as she lingered at the door before leaving. "You won't find Jack and Emma have much to say," she warned her. "But they're hard workers and get things done, so I guess the professor is satisfied."

"I must see Professor Collins," Maggie said. "Do you know where he is?"

"In his office on the first floor," the girl told her. "It's the door on your right as you come downstairs. He usually works in there in the mornings."

"And the others?"

Bessie grimaced. "You mean that snooty Harriet and the two professors who are helping? They never leave the cellar. At least not for very long. They've got cases and cases of weird things Professor Collins brought from Egypt to unpack."

"I know," she agreed. "It's a tremendous task."

The maid left her and Maggie hurriedly unpacked her things, dividing them between the closet and the dresser. Then she went downstairs to report to Professor Collins. The door to his office was closed, so she knocked on it.

"Yes?" came in a questioning, muffled voice from inside.

She took it as a summons to enter the room and did so. But his startled reaction made her realize he had merely intended for her to give him her message through the door. He'd been studying two breathtakingly lovely gold scarabs set with precious stones. Hastily he covered them with his hands and frowned at her.

Awkwardly, she explained, "I'm sorry I intruded. I merely wanted to ask you what you intended me to do."

"Ah, yes," Anthony Collins said with a wary look on his lined face, his hands still protectively hovering over the priceless scarabs. "I'm studying some imitations of the original scarabs that were taken from me by the Egyptian officials. I hope to use these to simulate the real ones when I put the collection on display. But I haven't decided yet whether they are good enough."

"I can come back later if you like."

"No. That won't be necessary," he told her. "You can go down and work with Herb Price. This afternoon you'll be with me as usual."

She hastily left him, feeling that she'd annoyed him by bursting in on him as she had, and found her own way down the rickety steps to the dank and dismal cellar rooms. They were as uncomfortably chilly and poorly lighted as on her first visit. She passed through the first room with its stacks of wooden cases and in the second room came upon the elderly Professor James Martin. The scrawny old man was on his knees beside an uncrated stone tablet on which was carved a scene of herdsmen driving their cattle.

His pallid face was upturned to her now. He said, "You're the young woman Anthony hired yesterday, aren't you?"

She smiled. "Yes."

"See this," the old man said proudly, pointing at the tablet before him. "Art as ancient as this and in this state of preservation is rare. It's worth any risk to bring it back."

Her eyebrows raised. "Any risk? You think there is a risk?"

The old man shrugged. "You have heard of the curse?"

"Yes."

"Lord Carter was a personal friend of mine," the old man said, still on his knees. "He financed the original expedition and he died of a mosquito bite. Some rare disease was transmitted to him by the insect. A few say it was a disease that went back to the time of Rehotip."

"Did he get the bite while at the site of the tomb?"

The elderly professor nodded. "Yes. I have read part of the inscription on the corridors of the tomb: 'I place thy might and the fear of thee in all lands, and the terror of thee as far as the four supports of the sky.' There's a lot more. I'm not a superstitious man but it makes you wonder."

"I suppose so," Maggie said. Fearing Professor Collins might come down and find her still not at work, she excused herself and went on. In the fourth and largest of the rooms she found Professor Price and Harriet Fennel busy making notes on several exquisite vases in various shades of clay which they had on the desk by them. They were laughing and talking in an intimate manner as they went on with this task. Maggie felt so much like an intruder in the murkily lighted room that she was blushing.

Harriet noticed her first. "Well?" she asked.

"Professor Collins told me to come down and assist Professor Price."

Herb smiled a greeting, showing no ill results from the attack he'd suffered in the storm the previous night. "Good morning."

Harriet frowned. "If you're to work here I may as well get on to something more useful." And she turned accusingly to the young professor. "Did you ask for Miss Evans to help you? I understood she was to be Anthony's helper."

Herb Price looked amused. "She is. But in the afternoons only since Professor Collins does his office work in the mornings."

"I hadn't thought of that," Harriet agreed, in somewhat better humor. She told Maggie, "He'll tell you what to do." And she strode out of the room, leaving her alone with Herb Price.

The first thing he did was apologize for the previous night.

"I'm sorry I left you so abruptly," he said. "But I was in terrific pain."

"It didn't matter," she told him, putting on one of the gray smocks.

He still looked contrite. "I worried about you getting to Collinwood."

"I made out very well," she said. "By the way, just after you left me I heard the cry of a wolf. Did you hear it?"

The young professor looked uneasy. "I can't say that I did."

"It struck me as odd, since you'd mentioned there might be wolves in the area. Yet it's only since we've met that I've heard them."

He avoided looking at her directly, giving his attention to setting down some details about one of the vases in his notebook. At the same time he casually said, "Probably I put the idea in your head. I'm sorry. You probably became panicky alone in the storm and imagined those wolf calls."

"I don't think so," she protested. "They were real."

"Could have been some dog lost in the storm," he said, putting down his notebook and giving her a partial glance. "The night was bad enough to make anything howl."

"That's true," she said, studying him. "Do you feel better?"

"Yes. As soon as I got back here and took my medicine I was fine."

"Are you often subject to such seizures?"

He spread his hands. "I can never tell. The heart specialist I talked with claimed I could go for years without one. Then I might get three in a week."

She frowned with concern. "Are they considered dangerous?"

"It's more a chronic condition," he said. "Shall we get down to work? There are some small pieces in that opened crate. Lift them out one at a time and carefully place them on the desk with the vases. I'll examine them and list the details about them."

She went to the large crate and reached into its shadowy depths to remove a squat vase and place it on the desk before the young man. She gave him another appraisal, as he in turn concentrated on studying the vase, and again she was struck by the familiar look about him. She was sure she'd either seen him or his photo somewhere.

"All taken care of," he informed her as he finished writing in his notebook with a flourish. "Next."

She bent over the open crate again, reaching into the darkness of its interior to make contact with the smooth surface of what seemed to be a plate. She used both hands to carefully lift it out. Suddenly she was horrified to feel something cold and slimy move against her wrist. With a scream she let go of the plate as she recoiled in horror from the thing deep in the dark crate.

CHAPTER 4

Professor Price came rushing quickly to her side. Lending an arm to offer her support, he asked, "What is it?"

She pointed to the crate. "In there. Some dreadful slimy living thing. It crawled over my hand!"

He gave her a concerned look. "Stand away from the crate," he ordered her. He went back to the desk and picked up a flashlight. Returning to the crate he shone it on the dark bottom where the remaining clay pieces were. "I don't see anything," he finally announced, glancing up at her.

Still in a state of shock, she insisted, "There has to be something. I felt it."

His expression was grim. "We'll see," he said. And he began probing around in the crate with the flashlight.

"I think it was some sort of small lizard," she hazarded.

The young professor suddenly leaned back from the crate. "You're right," he agreed. "It was hiding inside one of the vases. I just drove it out now. It's a lizard of a species I've never seen before."

"Could it be poisonous?"

"Very likely." He frowned. "It didn't sting you, did it?"

"No, I pulled away as soon as I felt it," she said with a shudder, staring fearfully at the wooden crate. "What are you going to do with it?"

He frowned. "I'd like to save it to show Professor Collins. If he can't identify it, we could send it in to Boston. This could be a find—a lizard that's somehow managed to exist for thousands of years. It'd been curled up in one of the clay pieces when we packed them."

Maggie still kept her distance from the crate. "Isn't it liable to try to escape from in there?"

"No," he said. "They prefer the dark. Right now I'm looking for some sort of jar to hold it." He glanced at her. "Go ask Professor Martin to come in here."

"Will I tell him what happened?"

"You can." He was already opening a wall cabinet and searching its shelves for a suitable container for the lizard. Maggie hurried out of the room, glad to put some distance between herself and the crate with the tiny horror in it. She found James Martin seated at his desk in the second room.

"Professor Price wants you," she said hurriedly. "He's just come upon some sort of lizard in one of the packing boxes. Or rather I found it first. It ran across my hand."

The frail old man was at once on his feet. "Did it sting you?"

"No."

His parchment-pale, lined face showed concern. "Are you sure?" And then coming up to her, he asked, "Which hand?"

"The right one," she said, holding it out for him.

Professor Martin made a quick examination of her hand. "It seems you were lucky." Then he started on his way to the rear room with her trailing after him.

By the time they reached Herb Price he had captured the lizard and was triumphantly holding it up in a glass jar with a tight cover. "There you are, ladies and gentlemen," he said, mocking a side show barker, "positively the only one of its kind in existence!"

Professor Martin adjusted his rimless glasses and peered at the glass jar. The vicious looking green lizard inside it was about four inches long and had an ugly wide head that measured an inch at least. A darted tongue kept in constant motion as the lizard slithered wildly inside the jar.

Professor Martin shook his head. "I can't place it in any category," he readily admitted. He gave Herb Price a questioning look. "Do you suppose it could have actually come from the tomb?"

"Why not?" he said. "It could have been in any one of the vases."

Professor Martin's frail figure almost trembled with excitement. He pointed a thin forefinger at the jar. "That little fellow may have been placed in the tomb by one of King Rehotip's trusted servants. If so, the chances are it's poisonous. Some of the Egyptian kings used to pepper their tombs with all kinds of poisonous creatures to guard against the tombs being vandalized. If that's so in this case you can count yourself lucky, Miss Evans."

"I do," she said in a small voice.

Professor Martin looked at Herb. "I've always suspected the insect that poisoned Lord Carter and caused his death was no ordinary one, that it was linked with the curse of Osiris."

Herb still held the jar with the; weird captive in his hand. "If that should be true, we ought to be especially careful handling this stuff. The entire shipment may be loaded with poisonous creatures."

Maggie gasped. "Oh, no!"

"Don't be alarmed, young lady," the veteran professor said. "I doubt that we'll find much of anything in the other crates. But I agree precautions should be taken."

"What do you suggest?" Herb asked.

"We all should at least wear heavy rubber gloves when thrusting our hands into the crates. Anything less than that would be foolhardy."

"I agree," Herb said. "We'll halt operations here until we get the gloves and I'll take this jar up to Professor Collins and get his verdict."

"Be cautious with it!" the old man called after him. "We don't want a string of strange deaths in our group." Maggie was still standing there in the murky yellow light of the underground room. She gave the old professor a frightened look. "Do you really think that could happen?"

"Why not? Those Egyptians were devious people. And it might be possible for some of the poisonous creatures to remain in a state of inactivity for literally thousands of years and then come alive again."

The words of the old man troubled her. Even after Herb Price found suitable protective gloves for all of them, she approached the crates with fear. The day seemed to stretch out endlessly. Except for a short break for lunch they worked straight through. In the afternoon she assisted Professor Collins, but her work was the same.

Anthony Collins regarded the discovery of the lizard as an important piece of luck. "I'm taking the lizard into Boston personally," he exulted. "I have every reason to believe that it dates back to the sealing of the tomb."

"You believe it is poisonous, and was placed in the tomb to protect it against intruders?"

"Definitely," Anthony Collins said with that wild gleam in his watery blue eyes. "It was most fortunate that you came upon it."

"I'm still frightened."

"Don't think about it," was his advice as he began cataloging a necklace which she'd placed before him.

At last night came. The members of the group had dinner at a large community table. The three professors hazarded theories as to the origin of the lizard. Maggie found the discussion upsetting, and even Harriet silently indicated annoyance at the enthusiastic comparing of notes.

Maggie was astounded by the complete preoccupation of these people with Egypt and the tomb of King Rehotip. It was as if nothing else of importance existed. Not only was the house filled with crates holding the bulk of the long dead king's treasured belongings but all the waking hours of the group seemed dedicated to study and talk of Egyptology. She longed for the free atmosphere of Collinwood.

And she began to wonder if she hadn't made a mistake in coming to the old red brick house. She went to the living room window and looked out at the snow-covered hills. The frigid winter night outside was a far cry from the atmosphere in the house.

The three professors had gathered in the study for a talk. Harriet had excused herself to go to her room. She had obviously been anxious to snub Maggie on her first evening in the house and this had been her method of doing it. Maggie stood alone by the living room window in a depressed state of mind.

Then the front door knocker sounded and she went to answer the door. And her heart gave a great leap of delight as she saw that it was Barnabas standing there.

"I'm so glad to see you, Barnabas," she said, "please come in."

He entered, his silver-headed black cane in hand and a grim smile on his face as he noticed the crates cluttering up the room. "You have some odd pieces of furniture here," he teased her.

She smiled. "Packing cases are everywhere in the house except the bedrooms."

"It's a very cold night."

"I guessed that," she said. "Though in here everything is Egypt. Please sit down."

They sat together on a small divan and she gave him a hasty account of her day, giving particular attention to the episode of the lizard. The gaunt, handsome man listened with deep interest. When she had finished, he said, "I don't like that lizard business. There may be more danger in that line."

She smiled at him ruefully. "I'm beginning to think your advice was good. This is something I should have skipped."

"You can leave whenever you like," he reminded her.

"I tell myself that," she agreed. "It helps keep me from complete panic."

"What about that young man whose face seems familiar to you? Did he give you a proper explanation for leaving you so suddenly last night?"

"No. Oh, he said something about medicine being here and his having had similar heart attacks in the past."

Barnabas raised his heavy dark eyebrows. "Oh, he blames it on his heart?"

"Yes. I mentioned the wolf I'd heard and he suggested I must have imagined it because I was afraid."

"Do you agree with that?"

"No. I did hear some kind of howling."

Barnabas sighed and tapped a crate with the tip of his cane. "This house and the people in it would make a fascinating study for me if you weren't exposed to it all."

"Am I truly in danger, do you think?"

"I'd rather see you at Collinwood," was his quiet reply. Just then the tall, thin figure of Anthony Collins appeared in the doorway of the living room. On seeing Barnabas, his scholarly face took on an expression of mild annoyance. He came forward.

"Barnabas Collins," he said. "I had no idea you were in Collinsport or that you were a friend of Miss Evans."

Barnabas rose and held out his hand. "I count myself fortunate on both scores. It has been a long time since our last meeting, Cousin Anthony."

The dour professor shook hands with him gingerly. It was plain that he was no admirer of Barnabas. He asked, "What are you doing back here?"

"I have come to be with the family for the Christmas festivities," Barnabas said affably.

Anthony eyed him dubiously. "I should have thought you wouldn't be in a hurry to return here after the unpleasantness during your last visit."

"I've never felt that way about Collinsport," Barnabas said. "It is our family home and I always anticipate my visits here."

"You look very well. I trust you are enjoying your usual health."

"My usual health," Barnabas said evenly. "And I hear you have defied the curse of Osiris and the good King Rehotip to bring back all the treasures I see created around me." He indicated the boxes cluttering the room.

Anthony smiled coldly. The watery fanatical blue eyes showed a gleam of sheer hatred. "Unlike you, my dear Barnabas, I have no fear of the supernatural. I do not regard the ancient tombs of Egypt as sacred. My position is that their contents offer valuable material for the knowledge of mankind's beginnings."

"Still, the tombs are graves and you are robbing them."

For an instant, Anthony's anger was obvious, but he

quickly controlled it. "I can not expect you to hold the views of an Egyptologist, my dear Barnabas. I must consider you limited in that area of culture."

Barnabas' gaunt face showed no expression. "I have a great respect for the dead," he said quietly. "And for their resting places."

Anthony Collins looked taken back by the quiet sincerity of the remark. Then, eyes flashing angrily, he snapped, "I had almost forgotten. But your preoccupation with the dead is a natural thing. True to your nature."

"That's a matter of debate."

"Not so far as I'm concerned," the professor said coldly. "I'll wish you goodnight." And to Maggie, he added, "I'll see you in the morning, Miss Evans. I trust you rest well in your new bedroom."

"It seems very comfortable," she told him. "I'm positive that I will."

Anthony Collins nodded curtly and then strode out of the room. They could hear him mounting the stairs to his bedroom. Maggie gave a sigh of relief at his going.

She asked Barnabas, "Why should he say that about your being interested in the dead because it was true to your nature?"

He shrugged. "Don't ask me to explain all the fuzzy thinking of my elderly cousin," he said. "He is very narrow in his views, as you must have noticed."

"I have," she worried. "And it seems clear that Roger made no mistake when he said that you and Anthony don't get along well. You were both fairly bristling at each other."

Barnabas smiled. "I'm not concerned that he dislikes me. We are miles apart in our thinking. It is natural."

"Don't come here for my sake if it makes you uncomfortable," she said. "I'll gladly go up to Collinwood for our meetings if you'd rather."

"Just don't worry about it."

At that moment Professors Martin and Price came into the room. Maggie quickly introduced them to Barnabas. It seemed to her that Herb Price flinched at the sight of Barnabas.

They showed no interest in remaining to talk, and when the two professors had also taken the stairs to the second floor she found herself alone with Barnabas again.

She asked in a low voice, "What do you make of Professor Price?"

His brow was furrowed. "Of course he is the one you felt you had seen before."

"Yes."

"It is quite possible you have. If not in person, at least in a photograph."

She was puzzled. "But where and when?"

Barnabas glanced in the direction of the stairs and then in a low voice, asked, "Surely you've heard of Quentin Collins?"

Maggie considered. "The name is familiar."

"He's another of the family who shows up here at intervals. There have been whispers that he has involved himself with witchcraft. Some think he is under the curse of the werewolf."

Remembrance at once came back to her. She had heard these rumors and paid little attention to them. And Elizabeth had showed her a picture of Quentin Collins in the album of photographs of the family.

She stared at Barnabas. "Of course, he does bear a remarkable likeness to Quentin. But his hair is lighter, and he wears glasses."

"Glasses and hair dye are simple means of disguise," Barnabas said quietly. "I'm by no means sure that your Professor Herb Price is Quentin back here under an assumed name. Just the same I'd watch him closely. Especially since there is the wolf business involved."

Maggie's eyes reflected her fear. "He did bring up the subject of wolves. And then there was that weird experience of last night when he fled from me and I heard the wolf calls later."

"Significant under the circumstances," Barnabas said. "I'll take the trouble to check some New York sources and see what I can find out about the background of Professor Herb Price."

"I wish you would," she said. "Shouldn't Anthony Collins have recognized him if he really is Quentin?"

"Not necessarily," Barnabas said. "Anthony is of another generation. And he's been away so much, he wouldn't be as well informed on Quentin as we are."

"Why should Quentin want to come back here?"

Barnabas smiled bleakly. "That might prove an interesting story in itself. But we mustn't forget it was once his home. And just as I enjoy coming back to the place where the family began, so might he."

"Yes, I suppose so."

"Just be extremely cautious," Barnabas said. "And if there are any new complications, send word to me at the old house. If I'm occupied in the daytime, as I almost invariably am, Hare will take the message and give it to me when I'm available."

She smiled wanly. "You're still working on your book?"

"Yes. Most of my days are devoted to research and writing," he said. "Now I really must go and allow you to retire. Otherwise Anthony will be coming downstairs and ordering me out."

Maggie shook her head. "He wouldn't dare do that. It was good of you to come. And I will be careful of Professor Price until we're more sure about who he is." She saw Barnabas to the door.

"If I don't hear from you first I'll be by another evening," Barnabas promised. Then he kissed her goodnight and left.

She turned out the fights and went up to her room with a feeling of fear. There was a brooding atmosphere in the red brick house that worried her. It was as if the curse of Osiris had already settled on the house and the people in it.

Yet sleep came to her fairly soon, in spite of the strange bedroom and her ill-defined uneasiness. Her first sleep was sound. But she wakened after two and could not seem to doze off again. Outside the wind howled mournfully and the old house cracked from the frost every so often.

Later she was to decide her wakefulness was lucky, for while she was trying to induce sleep again a sudden noise alerted her. She raised up on an elbow and stared into the near darkness of her room at the sound of the door from the hallway slowly creaking open!

She stared at the moving door in the shadows with mounting terror. All the somber atmosphere of the mansion containing those crates filled with relics from an Egyptian tomb closed in on her. She recalled the curse of Osiris and the possibility that Professor Price was really the renegade Quentin. There was much to fear there!

Now the door was wide open and a shadowy figure stood in the doorway. She couldn't tell whether it was a man or woman; the outline of the apparition was blurred. But it came toward her slowly, filling her with apprehension. At the foot of her bed it made a kind of gesture, as if tossing something at her.

Instinctively she knew what it was. Even before the slimy thing came crawling across the bedspread she had seized a heavy glass ashtray from the bedside table. With screams of terror she struck out at it wildly and then fumbled for the switch on the bedside lamp. She found it and turned it on, panting with terror. Her aim had been better than she could have hoped. The battered remains of the lizard made an ugly stain on the bed covering.

In the dreadful moment of defending herself from the obscene thing the ghost figure had vanished. And now the first person to show himself in the doorway was Professor Herb Price, wearing a bathrobe and looking sleepy. The young man entered the room and came over to her bedside. "What's happened?"

She mutely pointed to the bed cover as she swung out of bed and threw on a robe. The young man saw the remains of the lizard and a shadow crossed his pleasant face.

"How did it get in here?"

"Someone brought it."

"Someone brought it?" he echoed incredulously.

She nodded. "A ghostly figure came into the room and tossed the lizard on my bed!"

At this time Professor Collins arrived in pajamas and dressing gown. He came over to them with a troubled look on his lined face. "What was all the screaming about?"

Maggie pointed to the bed covering. "That!"

Anthony Collins gasped. "What does this mean?" he demanded angrily. "How did the lizard get in here and why did you destroy it? It might have been the find of the expedition."

"I had to protect myself." She told him how the lizard had come to be there.

The old professor scowled. "This specter you claim entered the room, surely you must be able to give us some description of it?"

"I'm sorry, I can't," she said unhappily. "It was a shadow. Only that."

Herb Price turned to his senior colleague. "The room was in darkness and Miss Evans was naturally badly scared."

Anthony Collins was staring at the ugly spot on the bed again and murmuring. "Lost! One of our most valuable finds!"

Behind the heavy glasses, Herb's eyes blazed with indignation. "The important thing is not that the lizard was destroyed but that Miss Evans managed to kill it before it stung her fatally."

The older man looked chagrined. He waved a hand impatiently. "Miss Evans surely understands that I regard her safety first. Still, it is a calamity that this valuable specimen should be destroyed."

"Where were you keeping it?" the young professor asked.

"I turned it over to my secretary," Anthony Collins said. "I asked her to be responsible for it and keep it in the closet with some other specimens in her room. I was taking some of these things to Boston in the morning." Maggie knew that Harriet resented her and was obviously extremely jealous of her joining the group, but she hardly gave her credit for this weird attack. "Somebody must have stolen the thing from Miss Fennel's room."

Herb Price nodded. "Very likely."

"I wonder where she is, and Professor Martin?" Anthony Collins fretted.

Herb smiled grimly. "Considering his age and deafness, I'd guess Professor Martin is still asleep. I can't imagine that Harriet hasn't heard the commotion."

At that moment Harriet Fennel came through the doorway, followed by the pretty maid, Bessie Miles. They were both in dressing gowns and Bessie looked frightened.

Anthony Collins told Harriet, "We've been wondering where you were." To Bessie, who'd remained sleepily in the background, he said, "Change this bedspread for Miss Evans. It's been soiled."

As Bessie came forward to do this, Harriet Fennel asked,

"What happened?"

Anthony Collins told her the story, ending plaintively, "I never expected anything like this to take place. I was sure you'd give the lizard excellent care."

Harriet Fennel flushed guiltily. "I don't see how I can be blamed. One doesn't expect thieves or madmen in the house. And this must be the case unless Miss Evans had some kind of nightmare."

Maggie nodded to the spread which the maid was removing. "It was no nightmare."

Professor Collins stood there glumly, looking more elderly than in his usual daytime clothing. The slight stubble of gray beard on his face gave him a haggard appearance. He sighed heavily. "I don't understand this ghost business."

Professor Price looked just a trifle guilty as he stood there staring down at the carpet and avoiding the eyes of the others. He was being strangely subdued for him, Maggie thought.

Harriet said, "I'd think any further investigation can wait until the morning."

Price said quietly, "It might be wise to check on the jar in which the lizard was being kept. This could have been another one."

Anthony Collins' glum face took on a new light of hope. "I hadn't thought of that," he said excitedly. "Let us check on the jar at once."

Led by Harriet, they all trooped out of the room and down the shadowed hallway. The closet door was still partly open; the jar lay on the floor on its side. Empty! "That settles that," Anthony Collins said dejectedly.

Harriet Fennel gave Maggie a sullen glance. "Perhaps Miss Evans is a sleepwalker and doesn't know it. She might have released the lizard from the jar herself."

"That's utter nonsense!" Maggie said hotly. "I've never had any sleepwalking problems. And I'd certainly not bring the creature to my room in any case."

"That is true," Anthony Collins observed. "It was Miss Evans who was threatened. We mustn't blame her."

Harriet's eyes blazed with contained anger. "I find her account of a shadowy figure a bit too much! I for one don't believe in ghosts!"

Professor Herb Price gave her a glance of reprimand. "You might do well to remember there are three caskets in the cellar containing the bodies of King Rehotip and two of his court. And there is the curse which we have defied. Taken together, they seem to spell the possibility of supernatural influence to me."

Anthony Collins bridled. "Utter rot! I see nothing to be gained by discussing this further. We may as well return to our beds and talk about it in the morning."

They dispersed, going their separate ways back to their bedrooms. Herb Price remained with Maggie, as his room was down the hall opposite hers. At her door he paused to reassure her. "I don't think you'll be bothered again." Shivering she glanced into her own room. The bedcover had been replaced and the maid had gone.

She said, "What I told them was true. There was a figure! A ghostly figure!"

The young professor looked at her oddly. "Expect people to be skeptical of such stories," he warned her. "You may have imagined the ghost even though the lizard was real enough."

"Then how did it get into my room?"

"If it was released from the jar it might have easily wandered in any direction. It just happened to head for your room."

Maggie's face showed disdain. "You're stretching coincidence too far."

He shrugged. "It's not likely anyone in this house would let that possibly valuable specimen escape."

"I suppose not," she was forced to agree.

The stern eyes behind his heavy glasses met hers. "If there was a figure, it must have been that of an intruder. Someone may have gotten into the house and done this." She frowned. "That isn't likely."

"As likely as any other theory," he said. "Even more so. Goodnight."

She went into her own room and closed the door. There was no lock on it, not even a latch. So she took a plain chair and braced it against the door, still thinking over Herb Price's final suggestion that an intruder might have been responsible. And she worried that he had been subtly referring to her own visitor of the evening, Barnabas Collins!

CHAPTER 5

The following morning was cheerless gray without any promise of sun. Maggie went down to breakfast in a depressed state of mind. Her eerie experience of the night before and the generally ominous atmosphere of the red brick house had about decided her that she should give up this new job and return to Collinwood.

At the breakfast table she found Professor James Martin. The frail old man greeted her with a smile. "Ah, Miss Evans, I hear you had a most unpleasant thing happen to you last night."

She took her place opposite him. "It was like a nightmare."

He nodded thoughtfully. "Shocking, I agree."

The maid came to silently wait on them and Maggie told the professor, "I don't think I'm suited for this work. I believe I should tell Professor Collins so and leave."

He looked concerned. "I trust you haven't arrived at this decision rashly. You may never have such an experience again. And we do need your help here."

She sighed. "I'm not sure I'm in agreement with what you're doing. Even though you open these tombs in the name of historical research, you are actually robbing graves, aren't you?"

The old man looked startled. "That's a primitive way of putting it," he said. "I've never regarded it in that light. Ours is not an easy profession, Miss Evans; it requires dedicated men. I have lost my health through explorations. The malaria from which I suffer keeps coming back and robbing me of a little more of my strength each time. And the best experts assure me it is incurable."

"But you consider what you have accomplished has made the sacrifice worthwhile?"

Professor James Martin nodded. "I must believe that and so must the others."

"And so you braved the curse of King Rehotip?"

A humorless smile flickered across the old man's sallow face. "Not without being fully aware of the risks. A number of people associated with the first expedition who lost their lives were friends of mine. I prefer to think the curse of Osiris had nothing to do with their deaths."

"But the possibility remains," she said quietly.

"I cannot deny that, but I beg you to give this matter your keenest judgment. And before you make any definite decision, talk the whole thing over with Professor Collins."

"I will do that."

But her mind was made up. When she finished breakfast she went up to the second floor and sought Professor Anthony Collins out in his office. He listened to her side of things with striking patience.

When she finished, he said, "I'm going to offer you several thoughts. And I trust you won't resent what I say."

"I try to keep an open mind," she said with a small smile.

"One cannot ask for more," Anthony Collins said, his pale blue eyes fixed on her as he sat at his desk. "Last evening you had a visitor."

"I did."

"Barnabas Collins is no stranger to me," the old man went on. "And I imagine you've guessed he is no favorite of mine."

"I felt that when you met."

"Just so," the professor said curtly. "I dislike speaking against a friend of yours, but do you have any idea of the history of this man?"

"Only that he has traveled a great deal."

"True enough," Anthony Collins said. "He has been a wanderer. And with a reason. I doubted he would ever return to Collinwood with the police still suspicious of him."

"Why should they be interested in Barnabas?"

Anthony Collins leaned forward to her. "You have surely heard of the vampire legend associated with the history of Collinwood?"

Maggie hesitated. "Yes, I have. Most everyone knows the story. Years ago, the first Barnabas Collins was supposed to have fallen under the spell of a witch from the West Indies, a lovely young woman named Angelique. As a result of the curse placed on him this first Barnabas became a vampire."

"Those are the exact details," the thin man agreed. "Which brings us down to the present. A good number of people, including many of the villagers, give credence to the theory that the curse has been passed down over the years. And that this present Barnabas is also tainted by the vampire, thing."

"But that's preposterous!"

He spread his hands. "Don't be too quick to say so, Miss Evans. You might have reason to change your mind."

"I can't think that I will."

"More unusual things have happened," the professor commented dryly. "I have only mentioned this because you were the one who brought Barnabas Collins into the house last night. And who can say that he didn't return later ... as the spectral figure you saw?"

"No!" she protested, jumping up.

The stern face before her was a warning. "I believe that is what happened. Barnabas wishes to frighten you away from here and also interfere with my work."

"Why should he want to harm you?"

"Because he believes I know his secret and he hates me for it," the professor went on quickly. "When he was at Collinwood before, a number of village girls were attacked and later found wandering with odd red marks on their throats. The police finally narrowed the suspects down to Barnabas. And before they could pin the attacks on him he vanished."

"I'm sure you're all wrong about him."

"Then why did he run away?"

"It might have had nothing to do with the attacks you mention," she pointed out. "From all I know about Barnabas, he is a quiet, moody man who often does things on impulse. He may simply have tired of Collinwood and made up his mind to leave suddenly."

"I would say that it was fortunate for him that he did," Professor Collins said grimly. "I dislike placing all this before you, but I want to prevent you from doing anything reckless."

"I'm in no danger of that."

"I hope not," he said. "But all I have told you about Barnabas is based on my own knowledge. And now that he has returned to Collinwood it wouldn't surprise me if the mysterious attacks on girls began once more. Just wait and see."

"Barnabas is my good friend and a fine man," she insisted, vaguely recalling some of the rumors she'd heard about him.

Elizabeth had talked about the gaunt, handsome man many

times. She'd discussed his fondness for the hours after dark, and how it had been his strange habit to visit the family cemetery at midnight and later. These things had been the subject of gossip in the village.

The Collinsport people recalled the dark shadow over his ancestor's past and linked him with the original Barnabas Collins. But, as Elizabeth had pointed out, this was as ridiculous as linking a modern descendant of someone who'd been accused of witchcraft in Salem centuries ago with the ancient witch. To call Barnabas a vampire was to be narrow and ignorant.

Anthony Collins rose from his chair and took a stand in front of her. "You could be right in your high opinion of Barnabas, though I frankly say that I don't share it. We'll forget that for the moment. But I do want to assure you we're engaged in work of importance here. Work that goes far beyond what Barnabas contemptuously referred to as grave robbing."

"He is entitled to his opinion."

"I'll not deny that," Anthony Collins said, the fanatical pale blue eyes studying her. "Losing that specimen last night was a distinct disappointment to me. But fortunately I have something even more important to count on."

"I'm glad."

"A first in Egyptology that could make me famous," the professor went on rather excitedly. "My name may go down in history for my work in recovering the King Rehotip treasures." He paused. "You saw the magnificent golden scarabs with their jeweled bodies which I had on my desk yesterday."

"Yes," she said. "I found it hard to believe they were merely imitations. They looked rich enough to be the originals."

He nodded grimly. "The native craftsman I hired when we found the holy beetles made remarkable copies of them before the Egyptian authorities demanded the originals for their country's museum. Only an expert could tell the difference."

"I'm sure of that."

"Few people know of the incident," he warned her. "Not even my colleagues here. So I'll depend on your silence."

"You may trust me."

"Thank you," he said. "When the time comes for the full display of the treasures to be shown, I shall include the imitation scarabs and give the press an account of what happened to the originals. It will make an interesting story and help exploit our collection. Until then I want nothing said about them. But though the Egyptian officials did rob me of the scarabs, they let me leave the country with an even more valuable asset without knowing it. And that is what I hope will win my bid for fame."

She felt uncomfortably aware of his fanaticism. He could

think of nothing but the Rehotip treasures; everything else was influenced by that. She wanted to be free of this forbidding old man and the house with its ghostly wooden crates. The gray morning light coming into the long narrow room which served as his office was as bleak as her thoughts.

She said, "Why do you tell me all this?"

His pale blue eyes fixed on her. "Because you can help me."

"How?" She thought he was trying to impress her, to persuade her to stay on doing the routine work in which she'd been engaged. A wily trick.

"Tomorrow I am sending the others to Boston with a group of the items we have cataloged thus far. Both of the professors and Miss Fennel will be required to make a quick transfer of the various pieces to the vaults of the Boston Historical Museum. They will be away from here overnight."

She had no idea what he was leading up to. She said, "Yes?" and waited for him to continue.

His weird blue eyes glittered. "Tomorrow night I need your help. I don't want any of the others involved. I daren't chance them sharing the honor I feel sure will come to me. But you are an outsider. You are no threat to my name. So you shall have an opportunity to share in an experience denied to any other human being." He was actually trembling as he finished speaking. It was logical in a way, Maggie thought. If he had made some stupendous discovery he might not want the others to share the moment of its first revelation. It could be that one of the many crates still unopened in that dark cellar really did contain a fabulous treasure undreamed of even by the Egyptian authorities.

She told him, "You know I came to you this morning expressly to ask you to allow me to leave."

Anthony Collins nodded. "I realize that. And I'm begging you to remain. At least until after tomorrow night."

Maggie deliberated quickly. His description of the discovery had caught her interest. It was possible all that he had said was true. She had become mixed up in the rather gruesome business this far; perhaps she should see it through at least a few days more. "Very well. I'll stay."

He looked delighted. "I promise you you're making no mistake."

She regarded him ruefully. "I wish I could be certain of that." And she got up from the chair.

The professor saw her to the door, but before he opened it he again cautioned her, "Please promise me your silence on all we have discussed."

"Very well."

"Don't even mention it to Price or Martin," he warned her. "They are trustworthy men, but I'm not ready to share my news with them yet."

It was an ideal opportunity to ask him about Professor Herb Price, the man both she and Barnabas suspected might be Quentin Collins in disguise.

She said, "Are you completely sure about Professor Price?"

The pale blue eyes blinked at her nervously. "Why do you ask that?"

"I know he is new with you."

"That is so," the elderly man agreed. "I put an advertisement in several suitable magazines and he answered it. He seemed the best of those who offered."

"And you're sure about his credentials?"

Anthony Collins frowned. "They seemed genuine. Have you any reason to be suspicious of him?"

"The day he first arrived, he turned up at Collinwood," she said. "And he walked right into the house. I found him there and directed him here. And he lied to me, saying the housekeeper had shown him in."

Anthony Collins' stern face revealed a look of mild astonishment. "That's strange," he agreed. "But after all, it wasn't an important lie. He might have been embarrassed at having been too brazen in the first place and tried to cover it up."

"I've thought the same thing," she agreed. "Though it struck me he was more familiar with Collinwood than a stranger would be."

"You could have imagined that," he suggested. "But I'm glad you mentioned this to me. I'll take another look at the letters he sent me when applying for the position here. And I'll watch him closely."

"He may be perfectly all right."

"I understand," the professor said with one of his rare smiles. "I assume you'll be going down to work with him for the morning."

"Yes, I'll go down now."

She was still lacking in enthusiasm for the venture. And the dull light of the cellar rooms made her feel more gloomy. Professor James Martin and Harriet Fennel were working together listing and restoring small stone figures of the god Anubis and Bastet. Anubis had been carved as a jackal, the animal which prowled in Egyptian cemeteries at night. And Bastet was the cat goddess of joy.

Absorbed in their work, they paid no attention to her. In the back room she found Herb Price standing by the three coffin-shaped boxes staring down at them. As she entered he glanced her way. "You're late."

"I had to see Professor Collins for a moment."

"Oh?" he raised his eyebrows. "I had an idea maybe you'd

resigned after last night."

"I felt like it."

"I wouldn't blame you."

She smiled ruefully. "Any way I've decided to stay on a few days more at least."

Herb observed her carefully through those thick glasses. "I was interested in your visitor last night. Distinguished looking, if I may say so."

"You may," she said. "He's a cousin of Professor Collins. Surely you must have met him before." She was hoping to trick him into admitting he had.

But the young professor was playing it wary. He shook his head. "Not that I know of. Is he a guest at Collinwood?"

"No. He lives in the old house. It's only a short distance from Collinwood. And he has a man with him to cook and look after the house."

"A gentleman's gentleman! He does travel in style."

"He's very nice," she said. "I knew him when he visited Collinwood before."

Herb smiled. "I see he didn't lose any time renewing his friendship and I can't say I blame him." He nodded toward the three coffins. "I'm wondering about these."

"What about them?"

He was staring at them disconsolately again. "I would have expected the professor to have started with the coffins. The mummies of the king and his followers are the most important part of the collection. Instead he keeps digging out the small stuff and allowing these to wait. My curiosity is getting the best of me. I'd like to take a look inside these boxes."

"I suppose he has a good reason."

"Maybe and maybe not," Herb Price said with a shrug. "I don't know whether it's obvious to you or not, but Professor Collins is an eccentric."

She smiled. "I decided that long ago."

"And now I've confirmed it," the young professor joked, "Well, I suppose our three friends will have to wait on the whim of Professor Collins."

She was staring at the three coffins. "Which one contains the body of King Rehotip?"

"Probably the one in the middle," he said. "It's the largest. So that indicates it has the most ornate coffin."

Maggie gave him a wondering look. "Do you think the body will be well preserved?"

"They usually are," he assured her. "Though I've known a few exceptions. Do you have any idea the amount of care they took with embalming these fellows?"

"I don't know anything about it.".

"Their deluxe embalming for kings like Rehotip took at least several months. First they made an incision and removed the viscera—the heart, liver, lungs and intestines. They were installed separately in stone vessels called canopic jars, each consigned to the protection of a particular god. But the heart was always placed back in the body because the Egyptians regarded the heart as the key to intelligence rather than the brain."

She smiled. "Maybe they had the right idea."

"Maybe," he said. "Anyway, the corpse was allowed to soak for around two months in a bath of niter, after which it was removed, dried and wrapped in strips of resinous linen. But before wrapping the body, the embalmer placed linen pads under the skin of the corpse. He was able to fill out sunken cheeks and give an appearance of firmness to the limbs which, before wrapping, were adorned with fine jewelry and ornaments."

"They went to a lot of trouble."

"They wanted their dead to be ready for the next world," he told her. "And now I suppose we'd better uncrate our share of jugs and vases or we'll be accused of wasting our time."

So they began a routine closely following the previous morning. Maggie carefully kept on her heavy rubber gloves when probing in the crates, not wanting a repeat of the nightmarish experience with the lizard. The time passed quickly. Soon the afternoon arrived; once again Maggie worked with Anthony Collins.

He appeared in better humor and as they worked he kept telling her interesting anecdotes of his many pilgrimages to the Middle East. She relaxed more than she had since she'd been in the red brick house. And the fact that Harriet Fennel remained cold to her didn't bother her at all.

It was dark when they left the cellars at the end of the day. She showered and changed into a smart suit of dark green for dinner. After dinner she found herself alone in the living room with Herb Price. Harriet Fennel had gone upstairs to write some letters and Professor Collins was in his second floor office, briefing Professor Martin on the moving of many of the pieces to Boston the following day.

Maggie and the young professor sat in a love seat before the blazing log fire in the fireplace. He smiled at her and said, "I wish you were coming to Boston with us tomorrow. I'll have the night free to enjoy the town."

She had a twinkle in her eyes. "You'll also have Harriet Fennel along."

"Harriet isn't much fun," he said. "You must have noticed that by now. She's an expert at sulking."

"I'll be busy here," Maggie said. "The professor plans to get a lot of work done while you're away."

"I wouldn't be surprised."

She sighed. "I wonder if it's very cold out. I should take a walk up to Collinwood and see David."

"Roger's son," he commented.

She gave him a surprised side glance. "You came up with that very fast. How could you know that David is Roger's son, since you're a stranger here?"

He looked embarrassed. "I haven't any idea. I guess Professor Collins may have mentioned it."

"He rarely talks about the family," she said, letting her doubt show in her tone.

Herb made an impatient gesture. "I heard it somewhere."

"I'm sure of that," was her dry comment.

He frowned at her. "Why do you pick me up on every little thing?"

"I don't mean to."

"You do," he insisted. "Since that first day we met at Collinwood you've given me the feeling you don't trust me."

"Sorry," she said lightly.

"I don't think you are." He got up and began to pace up and down nervously. "My nerves are bad tonight. I didn't mean to start an argument."

"But you often do."

As she finished speaking a distant howling came clearly through the winter night. On hearing it Herb Price came to a halt and stood looking straight ahead of him, his face pale and his eyes fear-stricken.

She said, "What's the matter?"

He stood there stiffly, not seeming to hear her. The wolf cry came once again. Nearer this time. He seemed frozen motionless. Maggie was startled at the change in him. She jumped up and took him by the arm. "Tell me, what's wrong?"

His answer was to shake free of her and turn to her with a strange light in his eyes. He seemed to be filled with an inner turmoil. "Don't bother me!" he said harshly.

"I want to help you!" she pleaded.

But he ignored her and rushed over to the stairs and up them. As he vanished she stood watching after him with troubled eyes. She went to the front door and opened it to check the cold. It was at least zero, but the night was clear with a host of stars overhead. The kind of night when you could walk in the snow and hear a pleasant crunching under your feet. She decided that she would take the time for a quick visit to Collinwood.

About ten minutes later she left the red brick house and walked up the road in the direction of the mansion. The plow had done its job well and so the walking was easy. She was warmly bundled against the cold and felt a glow of happiness when the distant lights of Collinwood came into sight.

With luck she might find Barnabas there along with Roger and David. This thought spurred her on at a faster rate. But when she reached the big house it was David who answered the door.

His boyish face showed a happy smile. "Maggie! I was hoping you'd come."

She laughed as she went inside. "I know you haven't really missed me."

"We all have," the boy insisted. "Dad said so at the table tonight."

"Where is your father?"

"He had to go back to the office. He left in the car about a half-hour ago but he said he wouldn't be late."

Maggie had taken her outdoor things off and she stood there feeling some disappointment. She'd hoped to have a talk with Roger. "Well, I have you to welcome me."

"And I do," he said. "Come into the living room and see how I've managed with my jigsaw puzzle."

She followed him into the living room and examined the partially completed puzzle set out on the hardwood floor before the fireplace. She knelt down with the boy and helped him fill in some additional pieces. It was a scene of ships in harbor.

As she worked, she asked, "Have you seen Barnabas?"

"Not since the first night he got here," David said. "But I was over to the old house this morning and Hare chased me away."

She gave the boy a warning look. "You shouldn't bother Hare. He has a bad temper."

"I know," David said. "My father says he's half-crazy."

"I don't think that's true," Maggie protested. "But he doesn't like people calling at the house in the daytime when Barnabas is writing."

"What about the ghosts?" David asked, his youthful face serious.

She gazed at him in amazement. "What ghosts?"

"The ones at the red brick house," David said solemnly. "I guess with all those coffins and things from Egypt you'd be bound to have some sort of spooks."

Maggie smiled grimly. "I'll be able to tell you more about them later."

She remained with the lad for an hour, but there was no sign of Roger or Barnabas. She began to feel uneasy about getting back to the other house, alone and on foot. She didn't want to leave too late. So she begged off from helping with the jigsaw and got ready to leave.

David saw her to the door. "When can I come down and see the coffins?" he asked.

"In a few days," she promised. "They'll be opened then and maybe Professor Collins will let you see the mummies."

"Boy!" David exclaimed, his eyes becoming large and round. As she started the walk back in the frosty night, she wondered where Barnabas was. He might be away from Collinsport. He sometimes made unannounced journeys, and he had spoken of getting further information on Herb Price.

Memory of that young man who she now felt was Quentin Collins in disguise bothered her. He'd too readily known who David was to be a complete stranger. But when he was seized by another of those odd spells, he had looked dreadfully ill and in pain. About that, at least, she was sure there had been no pretense.

If he was Quentin Collins, these attacks could be connected with the curse which tormented him. Rumor had it that during certain times when the moon was exactly right he became a werewolf.

A tiny shudder rippled through her as she gazed up at the full pale moon high in the star-filled sky. The gossip about Quentin, like the wild stories they told about Barnabas, had to be based on superstition and unfounded rumors. She didn't believe Barnabas was a vampire and she doubted that Herb Price, or Quentin, could change into a werewolf under a full moon.

She walked a little faster and soon she was nearing the red brick house again. Gray smoke was issuing from its chimneys and many lights glowed warmly in its windows. In a few minutes she would be safely inside.

The thought was still in her mind when from out of the bushes there came bounding a giant, snarling wolf. The terrifying creature blocked her path, its yellow eyes filled with mad hatred. At the sight of its powerful fangs she screamed and drew back!

CHAPTER 6

The bristling wolf was crouched, ready to spring. Frozen in unbelieving horror, Maggie waited for death. Then the headlights of an approaching car suddenly rounded a corner of the road from the direction of the village. As the two strong yellow beams of light illuminated the road the wolf gave up the attack and dashed back into the woods. It had all taken place within a few short seconds.

Maggie moved shakily to the side of the road as the car came up abreast of her. It was Roger's car. A moment later he swung open the door to question her.

"Did I see some sort of animal on the road with you a moment ago?"

She nodded. "A wolf," she said weakly.

"It looked like a big dog and then it made for the bushes," Roger said. "Get in for a moment and warm yourself."

Maggie was still sick from fear as she slid into the seat beside him and closed the door. "I don't know what might have happened if you hadn't come along."

Roger frowned. "It can't have been a wolf . . . though I admit it looked like one. Probably a mongrel dog that has strayed into the woods and is hungry."

"I don't think so," she said. "I've heard wolf calls in the night lately."

"There are no wolves in this part of Maine," he said flatly. "And if they keep roaring around the woods in those skidoos there won't be any animals of any kind left. I'll drive you down to the professor's."

"It's only a little distance now. I can walk."

"No," he said firmly. "You'll take no more chances tonight." As he drove ahead to find a place to turn, he asked, "Were you up to see David?"

"Yes."

"Good," he said. "We've missed you. But when you want to come again, phone first. I'll have a car pick you up and bring you back."

Roger drove to a place where the road had been widened enough to turn a car. Then he headed back to the professor's. Maggie was already finding it hard to believe what had happened. It seemed like another nightmare.

Roger asked, "How do you like the new work?"

"Not as well as I'd hoped," she confessed. "I may decide to give it up in a few days."

"Don't stay if you're not happy," he told her. "You've only taken the job to do him a favor."

"I'll let you know when I decide to leave."

"Do that," Roger said as he halted the car by the door of the red brick house.

"Barnabas hasn't been back to see you," Maggie said.

Roger looked grim. "No. And maybe that's just as well. I'm not happy about having him back here."

She gave him a searching look. "Did he really have some trouble with the police last time?"

He turned to her. "Where did you hear that?"

"Professor Collins said so."

Roger laughed harshly. "Depend on Anthony not to miss a chance to stab Barnabas in the back!"

"Is it true?"

"There were some nasty rumors."

"I'm sure there wasn't any truth in them," she insisted. "I think Barnabas is a fine man."

Roger gave her a mocking look. "A lot of girls think the same thing. The story goes that some of them wind up with strange marks on their throats."

"Meaning what?"

"Better ask Anthony," Roger said. "He can explain it better than me."

She said goodnight and went into the house resentful and troubled. Why were they all so against Barnabas? The lights were nearly all turned out in the red brick house. She silently made her way up the stairs. And when she reached the door of her own room she hesitated.

Herb Price's door was only a short distance down the shadowed hall. And she had a burning desire to know whether he was asleep or not. After debating with herself for a moment, she went down and knocked gently on the door.

There was no answer. Glancing up and down the hall cautiously to be sure she'd roused no one else, she repeated the knock. Still there was no reply. Now she very carefully gripped the knob and turned it slowly. She opened the door just a tiny bit, enough to see the bed hadn't been slept in and his room was empty. She closed the door again and hurried to her own room.

Once inside she braced a chair against the door. And then she went to the window and stared out a partially frosted pane at the winter night outside. The man she knew as Herb Price was surely not in the house. Was he somewhere out in the freezing cold, skulking in the forest? And had she been threatened by this same man, whose true name was probably Quentin Collins, in the guise of a werewolf?

It was a terrifying thought, but she remembered with relief that Professor Collins was sending Herb Price along with the others on the Boston trip tomorrow. It would give her some time to try to unravel some of the mystery surrounding the young professor's identity.

In the morning when she saw Herb Price he was getting ready to leave for Boston. He looked wan and tired, as if he'd had hardly any sleep. It seemed to Maggie that he tried to avoid her eyes as they talked.

She said, "When I came back from Collinwood last night I stopped by the door of your room to see if you were feeling better. But there wasn't any answer."

The young professor looked uneasy. "I went down to the kitchen to make myself a warm drink," he said. "You must have tried the door when I was down there."

She was certain this wasn't the truth, but she could hardly call him a liar. "That was probably it. So you are better."

"I'm feeling very well," he said with a hint of annoyance.

"Have a pleasant evening in Boston."

"I wish you were coming along." There was no enthusiasm in his voice.

Shortly afterward the trio left in the station wagon which had been loaded with items recovered from Rehotip's tomb. Professor Collins joined her in a jubilant mood, after waving them off. He said, "Now I must begin the preparations for our special task tonight."

Those bright, mad-looking eyes filled her with alarm. Suppose the Egyptologist was truly insane? What macabre business did he have planned for the night ahead? She daren't let herself dwell on the thought. "What do you want me to do today?"

"Nothing," he said. "I'd prefer that you rest for this evening. We'll likely be working until late."

Maggie made no comment. Deciding it would do no harm to learn a bit more about Egyptology, she found several books on the subject in the professor's library and settled down to some serious reading. The hours fairly raced away as she delved into the fascinating story of the pyramid builders. She read there had been taxes even in those days which were usually paid in kind with hides, labor or agricultural produce. And failure to pay such taxes could result in severe punishment.

Before she knew it darkness had settled. She and Professor Collins, who seemed highly nervous, were alone at the dinner table that night. He rambled on about the many wonderful things he'd done as an Egyptologist and suggested that before the night was over he might add fresh honors to his name.

When they rose from the table he told her, "Meet me in the large cellar room in a half-hour."

She put on her gray smock and made her way down the badly-lighted wooden stairway to the dank basement. It was strangely quiet down there and she began to have the same feeling of danger being near that she'd known on other occasions. Her good judgment told her she shouldn't be allowing herself to get involved with a fanatic. On the other hand it was a bare possibility that this cousin of Roger's might really be a genius.

When she reached the murky light of the largest room, she found the elderly professor on his knees beside the middle one of the three coffins, prying the wooden case open with an iron bar. Perspiration mottled his brow as he invited her to lend a hand.

She joined him on her knees and helped give leverage to the bar as they broke open the heavy packing case. After a few minutes he was able to swing back the top of the wooden coffin so she could peer inside and see the exquisitely carved golden casket. It was so utterly magnificent that she gasped in admiration.

Anthony Collins smiled triumphantly at her, those pale blue eyes more brightly insane than ever. "How do you like my surprise?"

"It's almost unbelievable!"

"This is only the beginning," he promised, running a greedy hand over the rich golden inlay of the coffin that had rested in darkness for several thousand years.

Awed, Maggie whispered, "The casket alone must be worth a fortune."

"And it must be turned over to the museum," he said sadly. "By the terms of my contract all such valuable items are to be donated to public institutions. The costs of the expedition have to be defrayed from the more ordinary pieces which we will eventually put up for auction."

"But you'll get the credit for the discovery."

His stern face relaxed. "Yes. I will get that." He looked at her with those weird eyes. "Now I have something to tell you which you may find hard to believe at first. So I beg you to take my word for it."

"I've already had to accept some strange facts."

"None stranger than what you will hear from me now," the elderly professor assured her. "It is why I had to get the others out of the way before I proceeded with the casket of King Rehotip."

"What are you trying to tell me?" she demanded, annoyed at his talking around the subject.

The mad blue eyes met hers. "The man inside this golden casket is not dead."

"Not dead!"

"That is what I said," he told her evenly. "King Rehotip is alive in there."

She automatically backed away from this positive proof of his madness. "But that can't be!"

"Don't think I'm insane," he begged her. "Let me explain."

"Go on."

"I'll have to fill you in on the background of this king so you'll understand properly."

She waited for him to continue. They were both kneeling beside the rough wooden box through whose top could be seen the fabulous golden casket inside. Above them the yellow light bulb dangled from its scraggly cord, highlighting the carved impassive features of King Rehotip and his folded hands. The dull light left most of the rough room with its earthen floors in shadows.

The professor took a deep breath. "The court of King Rehotip was as filled with traitors, as many another ruling house has been. The king was more than an ordinary devotee of Osiris, God of Death, and to win new fame for his favorite god and himself, he hit upon a plan to pretend he had died and been resurrected through the magic of Osiris."

"How could he do such a thing?"

"His plan was excellent. He had the court physician give him a mercury-like liquid which induced a coma resembling death. He'd already arranged with the physician and his heir and younger brother, Prince Seotris, to later give him an antidote which would restore him to life."

"And did they do it?"

"That is where the story becomes interesting," Anthony Collins declared. "Prince Seotris and the physician had been plotting to take the throne. The prince had no intention of giving his brother the potion to make him recover. Instead they decided to bury him and as a macabre joke place the potion in his casket with him."

"But they must have embalmed him according to the custom?

So he would surely be dead," she protested.

The old professor smiled craftily. "That is all explained in the scroll I found. It told every detail of the plot. The king was not dead so there was no need for embalming. They pretended to attend to it but it was not done. He was buried in a state of suspended animation. And he remains in that state this very moment!"

"It's fantastic!"

"But true. Now you understand why I have waited for this so long. Why I have to conduct this experiment without the others. But you shall share my moment of triumph!"

She stared at him incredulously. "You're not going to try and restore that poor body to life after all the time that has passed?"

"Why not?"

"You're doomed to failure," she said. "King Rehotip's plan was meant to cover only a short period of time. He's been in that coffin for thousands of years. Some deterioration of his mind or body has surely occurred."

Madness gleamed in the pale blue eyes of the Egyptologist. "I disagree," he said. "There should be no tissue change. And when the antidote is poured between his lips, King Rehotip should live again!"

"In a strange age and a foreign land of ice and snow! The shock of his returning to life should be enough to send him insane!"

"I don't agree," Anthony Collins said. "I have learned enough of the language spoken by him to be able to communicate effectively. Before this winter night is over the press and media people from the entire world may be beating a path to this isolated house. We'll cause a stir as great as man's conquest of the moon."

She listened to him with growing fear, aware that he believed all that he was saying. And she wondered if she could somehow escape from being part of the gruesome experiment. "Perhaps you had better try this alone."

"No! I must have a witness," he declared. "It's too late for you to refuse to help me now."

And he at once went about lifting the lid of the golden casket. A strange aroma of exotic spices mixed with a dusty odor of age assailed her nostrils. The mummified body of King Rehotip was revealed to them with the linen wrappings around it. Anthony Collins probed in the casket beside the body and after a moment produced a small glass vial with a purplish liquid in it.

"You see?" he said. "We have the antidote."

She shook her head. "You don't honestly plan to use it?"

"I most certainly do," he said coldly.

She had an almost irresistible urge to reach out and dash the vial from the old professor's hand so it would be broken and its contents spilled. But obsessed as he was with this scheme, he would probably kill her if she interfered at this time. She watched with horror as he carefully put the vial aside and turned his attention to unwrapping the linen strips covering the head and face of the long ago monarch of the Nile.

"Get me a larger pair of scissors," he ordered her curtly.

She brought them and again watched. Her tension grew as the glistening black hair of Rehotip was gradually revealed. And then the bronzed skin of his forehead came into view. The only sound in the dark cellar was Anthony Collins' labored breathing as he continued his macabre undertaking.

At last the head and shoulders of the long dead king were bared. Rehotip had a strong, sullen face—the face of one who has known complete authority and exercised it. His high cheek bones and sunken eyes were accentuated by his deathlike appearance. She could not believe that life still lingered in this thing of shrunken tissue.

Anthony Collins gave her a wild glance of excitement. "Now!" he said in a hoarse whisper.

It was like a kind of nightmare. She watched as he freed the stopper from the vial and with trembling hands brought it to the colorless lips of the corpse. At first the purple fluid spilled over the lips without entering the mouth. The professor uttered a low exclamation of annoyance and used his free hand to spread the lips apart slightly. The balance of the antidote dribbled into the king's mouth. Then Anthony Collins waited with his eyes fixed on the dead body.

There was no movement!

Maggie gave a deep relieved sigh. "I was sure nothing would happen after all this time."

His attention was still fixed on the motionless body in the golden casket. "The passage of years should have no bearing on the action of the drugs. A purely chemical reaction!"

"But you aren't dealing with something in a test tube," she protested. "This was a human being."

Anthony Collins continued to stare at the impassive features of King Rehotip, A shadow of disappointment was slowly gathering on his lined, pale face. "I have gambled my whole career on this," he murmured. "Risked the curse and all it could mean."

"You're lucky it's turned out this way," she said. "You still have a wonderful specimen of ancient embalming."

The professor looked at her blankly. "You're asking me to be happy about my failure?"

"I'm saying you should accept it," she told him. "You were expecting too much."

"I was the only man alive who knew Rehotip's secret. The possibility of his being brought back to life. And it has all come to nothing!"

"The expedition was successful."

Anthony Collins stood up and turned away from the casket. "Something must have happened to the antidote. I may have wasted too much of it when I spilled it just now."

Maggie said nothing for a moment. The dank gloom of the cellar room pressed in on her. Huge and distorted, the shadows of herself and the professor were outlined on the opposite wall in ghostly fashion. The room had taken on the odor of death.

Anthony Collins turned as if he were about to speak to her. Then, suddenly, there came a faint sound of movement from the golden casket. A chill shot up Maggie's spine. Unbelievably, the eyes of King Rehotip had opened. The dark brown eyes gazed straight up at the ceiling and had a wild light in them. She was too staggered to speak.

Anthony Collins' lined face had taken on an expression of sheer wonder. He was frozen motionless as he stared at the coffin. A weird shriek came from the lips of the bronzed figure in the coffin and there was the sound of ripping cloth as King Rehotip broke the linen wrappings that bound him.

In the next instant he had sprung to his feet. Most of his wrappings still clung to him in mummy fashion, though his head and shoulders were uncovered and his arms and legs free. He moved towards Professor Anthony Collins with an insane gleam in his eyes. Again a weird, savage cry escaped his lips and his bronzed, sinewy hands seized the professor's throat.

Anthony Collins tried to fight off the creature from the tomb without any success. Rehotip's stern face showed a savage pleasure as he brought the professor to his knees. Gasping for breath Anthony threw Maggie an appealing look.

She sprang forward and pounded the powerful Rehotip on the back and shoulders. It made no impression on him at all. But after a moment he let the professor's unconscious body slump to the floor and then turned on her. She screamed and backed away but he followed her relentlessly. Just as she was about to turn and make a break for the door, a clawlike bronzed hand reached out and seized her!

The glistening black hair and distorted bronze face came terrifyingly close to her. She could smell the foul breath of the ghoul as he drew her to him with those hands of steel! She screamed again and again as he twisted her arms tormentingly. Then with another wild, agonized shriek he hurled her away from him.

She spun back like a weightless figure and her head struck one of the packing crates. As the dark velvet of unconsciousness closed in on her she felt a surge of thankfulness. The horror had been too great to bear.

A moaning made her open her eyes. She was in a crumpled heap between two of the crates. Her head ached and reeled crazily so that the single light bulb suspended from the ceiling seemed to be a blurred half-dozen. She brushed the back of her hand across her forehead and tried to remember what had gone on. When it came rushing back to her, she uttered a whimper of fear. The moaning came again from somewhere near her and she raised herself up on an elbow to look around. It was Anthony Collins on his hands and knees by the golden casket, trying to stand. He seemed unable to summon the extra strength to rise to his feet. Blood was streaming down from a temple wound and spilling all over one side of his face.

Instantly forgetting her own misery, she grasped the side of one of the crates and helped herself up. "Just a minute, Professor Collins."

"He's gone!" the professor groaned. "Escaped!"

"I know that," she said grimly. "You can be thankful he didn't kill us before he left." And she took the old man by the arm and helped him to his feet.

"There was no warning," Anthony Collins wailed. "No warning at all. He came alive a madman!"

"I told you something like that might happen," she reminded him. With her handkerchief she wiped away some of the blood around his eye and on his cheek. The temple wound seemed superficial, though it was bleeding a good deal.

"Thank you," he murmured. "What about you?"

"Just a bump on my head and a general shaking up. The thing is, where did he go? Has he attacked any of the servants?"

Anthony looked alarmed. "We haven't heard any shouts from upstairs. We can hope the maid and Jack and Emma were in their rooms and so escaped him." He staggered weakly toward the door.

"Are you fit to walk yet?"

"Yes," he said tremulously. "I must find out what has happened, where he has gone!"

"I'll give you some support." She took his arm so that he could lean on her slightly.

In that fashion they made their way through the other rooms to the stairs. When they reached the upper hall they felt a blast of cold air. They moved on to the living room and found the door leading outside was wide open.

The professor looked stricken. "He's escaped from the house!"

"And he's insane!" she reminded him.

They went to the door and the odd footprints of the mad King Rehotip could be seen in the snow. They vanished in the direction of the road. Somewhere out in the wintery darkness the phantom figure of a man who had lived thousands of years ago stalked the unwary—Rehotip, still trailing his burial tapes and all powerful with the strength of the mad!

She closed the door and looked at the professor solemnly. "Do you realize what you have done?"

"I had no idea anything like this would happen!"

"That lost soul may kill any number of people until he's found and restrained!"

"I realize that."

"What are you going to do?"

The elderly professor shook his head. "I have no idea. He'll probably die from exposure. This snow and cold will kill him shortly."

Maggie frowned. "We're not dealing with a normal human being. This is a corpse revived after thousands of years. You have no way of knowing whether his body is any longer aware of heat or cold. Or whether it reacts to either."

"It will have to," he protested.

"You want to think that," she said accusingly. "But you may be wrong. Are you going to call the police?"

He looked frightened. "The police? What good would it do? They'll never believe me!"

"They'll have to if murders start being reported! Murders by a mad beast trailing a mummy's linen tapes!"

"Don't talk like that," he moaned, looking down.

"You have to face it," she said. "What are you going to do about reporting it?"

"Wait! He may be dead by now. We can try to follow his tracks and look for the body."

"The longer you delay reporting this, the more responsibility will be on your shoulders," she reminded him.

"Talking to the police will only cause trouble."

"You have to do something."

He touched a hand to his uninjured temple in a weary gesture. "What can I say?"

"Tell them the truth. That you revived a man dead thousands of years. Explain that he's escaped and is likely insane!"

"I can't say that," he protested. "No one will believe me!"

"A short time ago you were boasting of such an accomplishment, expecting the world to beat a path to your door!"

"But I didn't think anything of this sort would happen!" he said in an anguished tone.

"It has and you have a responsibility to the public." Their argument was interrupted by a knocking on the door. They looked at each other with wan faces for a long moment; then Professor Collins stepped to the door and turned the knob. Maggie held her breath as the door swung slowly open.

CHAPTER 7

Barnabas Collins was standing in the doorway. He bowed to the older man and came in to join Maggie. She felt relieved to see him feeling sure he would be of some help in this dread crisis.

The man in the caped coat stared at them. "You look as if you'd seen a ghost," he said. He turned to the professor. "What happened to your head?"

Anthony Collins regarded him grimly. "We've had a most regrettable accident here."

"So it would seem."

Maggie glanced across at the professor. "I don't know what you may have decided about the police but I think Barnabas must be told. We need advice from someone and who better can we find to give it?"

The professor hesitated. "I'm not sure it would be wise."

The gaunt, handsome face of Barnabas took on a look of mild astonishment. "I take it that I have intruded on something."

She looked up at him anxiously. "Something horrible has happened! We must have help."

Barnabas raised his eyebrows. "You sound very alarmed."

Anthony Collins cleared his throat nervously and approached his cousin. "I guess we may as well take you into our confidence," he said unhappily. "Less than a half hour ago I reactivated the body of King Rehotip. For more than two thousand years he lay in his coffin in a coma induced by drugs. I gave him a required antidote and he came back to the living state. But he returned as a pathetic madman."

"And a powerful one," Maggie said quickly. "He violently attacked both the professor and me before escaping. We're lucky to be alive."

Barnabas pointed his silver-headed cane at the front door. "Are you telling me this fugitive from the tomb is at large out there?" he asked quietly.

Professor Collins lifted his hands in a gesture of despair. "It was not my intention," he said. "I had no idea he would react in so wild a fashion."

Barnabas turned to Maggie. "Was anyone else involved in this?"

"Just myself and the professor," she said. "He waited until tonight to do the experiment, knowing the others would be in Boston. And by good fortune it seems the servants are safely in their rooms. He didn't disturb them. After he finished with us he found his way up here and outdoors. The door was open after him when we came upstairs."

Barnabas gave his cousin a bleak look. "Didn't you know better than to take such a chance? Was the warning of the curse of Osiris lost on you?"

Anthony eyed Barnabas surlily. "I did what any scientist or researcher in my place would have done."

"I wonder," Barnabas said dryly.

Maggie looked up at him with fear in her eyes. "I say we should tell the police. Don't you think so?"

"It would seem the easiest course," he agreed. "Though I doubt that they will be of much help to you. They probably won't even want to believe the story. The police in this area are singularly lacking in imagination."

Anthony Collins looked stubborn. "I say our best course is to keep quiet. To contact the authorities will only mean spreading a needless panic."

Maggie asked him, "What if that creature wanders about the countryside attacking innocent people?"

"That won't happen," Anthony Collins argued. "As I have told you before, King Rehotip will die in a short time from the cold."

Barnabas said sharply, "Wasn't he already dead? The state he is in now could scarcely be termed as alive."

Maggie nodded. "That's what I've told the professor. We're not dealing with a normal person and so you can't count on his minding the cold."

Barnabas turned to his cousin. "Well, Mr. Egyptologist, do you have an answer for that?"

Anthony Collins licked his lips nervously. "I still stay with my own theory. He will die in a few hours. His body will be found somewhere on the estate. Or perhaps he will fall into the ocean."

"That would be best," Maggie said. "Then there would be no need for awkward explanations."

"You're willing to risk that?" Barnabas said.

"Yes," Anthony said with a good deal of his former determination. "I have dedicated my life to the study of ancient Egypt. I believe I know the subject as well as any man."

Barnabas studied him with those deep-set eyes. "What do you know about the cult of the dead?"

"Enough. I have read many books on the subject."

Wry amusement showed on Barnabas' sallow face. "I think you may be about to learn more of the subject than you have ever read in books. And I warn you not to count on Rehotip perishing from the cold. I doubt that it will happen."

"Tomorrow morning should tell the story," was the professor's grim reply. "I will wait until then at least." He frowned at Barnabas. "I trust I can count on you for your silence."

"I will not interfere," Barnabas said quietly, "as long as your spectral fugitive refrains from killing wholesale. Then I might feel compelled to pass the information you've given me on to the authorities."

"If that happens I will tell them myself," Anthony Collins said. "I am not one to condone criminal action."

"Then we understand each other," Barnabas said.

The professor looked grim. "That is rare in itself."

Maggie suggested anxiously, "If King Rehotip isn't found by the morning, I say that Roger should be informed. This could mean danger for both him and David, not to mention the servants."

Anthony Collins looked unhappy. "He shall be told if we don't find the dead body of Rehotip by tomorrow. And now if you two will excuse me, I want to look after the cut on my head. And I badly need rest. You will look after locking the front door, Miss Evans."

"Yes," she promised. When the elderly professor had vanished up the stairs, Barnabas took her in his arms. Her head pressed close to him, she said, "What a dreadful night this has been!"

"It apparently didn't turn out as the professor expected."

She looked up at Barnabas in distress. "What could he have expected? I warned him there would be grave danger in what he was attempting. But he refused to listen."

"Warped ambition," he said bitterly. "And Anthony always has been a stubborn person."

"I should have taken your advice and left here at once."

He smiled at her. "If we all did the right thing at the proper moment, what a simple and uninteresting world this would be. I guess you did what you had to do. At least you've had an unusual experience."

Her eyes still reflected the horror of those moments in the shadows of the cellar as she told him, "It was as if he had returned from the dead. But I knew as soon as I saw his eyes and the expression on his face that he was violently insane."

"You mustn't dwell on it." Barnabas touched his lips to hers. After a brief embrace he led her over to the divan in front of the fireplace.

The lights in the room had been turned low and so the remains of what had been a healthy log fire provided most of the illumination. Barnabas' gaunt face took on a noble look in the flattering reddish glow.

She sighed. "I manage to control myself by thinking that it was a nightmare, that it really didn't happen."

"If that helps."

"But I know that it did!"

He frowned. "Why would he wait until you were here alone with him to conduct such a major experiment?"

Her smile was bitter. "Well, it was going to be a first in the field. And he feared that the others would attempt to rob him of some of the fame it would give him."

"So now the blame is entirely on his shoulders."

"I suppose so, though he'll probably find a way to avoid it. In many ways he is a devious character."

Barnabas smiled at her wanly. "In most ways, I fear. Anthony has never been one of my favorite relatives."

"And he hates you."

"Did he tell you so?"

She sighed again. "He didn't have to. He said things that were perhaps worse."

"Such as?"

"He brought up all that business about your ancestor, the original Barnabas."

"He would be bound to," Barnabas said grimly.

"Not content to let it rest at that," she continued indignantly, "he suggested that the taint had come down to you. That, you were cursed in the same way."

Barnabas stared into the waning fire, its warm light dancing on his sallow face. "I suppose he accused me of being a vampire."

"Yes."

"What did you say to him?"

"I told him I didn't believe it. I said that you were my friend and I wouldn't listen to such things said about you."

The gaunt, handsome face showed a sad smile as he turned to

her and took her hand in his. "That was kind and brave of you. But feel my hand. Doesn't it have the coldness of the grave?"

She shrugged. "Many people have cold hands."

"And when we kiss you must have noticed the chill of my lips?"

She looked at him with undisguised fondness. "I have come to like their caress."

He laughed softly. "You're in love with me, little Maggie. And love closes our eyes to all the unhappy truths."

"I do love you," she said. "And when you left me so suddenly that other time I was heartbroken."

Barnabas studied her with gentle eyes. "The parting had to be. To preserve our love."

She sighed. "I'm content that you are here. Please don't try to explain or make me see things differently. I'd prefer to be wrong than to be disillusioned."

"In that case I'll change the subject," he said lightly, "and move on to another one. I've made some inquiries by phone about your Professor Herb Price."

Maggie was at once interested. "What did you find out?"

"There are no records of an Egyptologist of that name in New York," he said. "From all that I have learned your young professor is a fake. And if Anthony had not been so desperately in need of colleagues he would have found this out through a simple check of his credentials."

"Should I tell Professor Collins?"

"I think not," he said. "Let us see what happens after Price returns from Boston. Sooner or later he is bound to reveal himself. But I have little doubt that he is actually Quentin Collins."

"He can be extremely likable."

"So can Quentin," Barnabas agreed. "It is not his fault that he suffers the werewolf curse. I know that he fights against it. But there come times when it is too powerful to contend with."

She shuddered. "Last night he had another of his spells. And later when I was on my way from Collinwood I was stalked by a giant wolf. I don't know what would have happened if Roger hadn't come along in his car and frightened it off."

"What did Roger say about it?"

"He was upset, but he didn't believe it was a wolf. He was convinced it was a wild dog desperate for food. But I was close to the snarling creature and it was a wolf!"

"If Quentin had one of his spells it could have been him. There was a full moon last night."

"Do you really believe such curses exist?" she asked incredulously. "When you are accused of being a vampire I put it down to people not knowing you. And to their ignorance and superstition.

Isn't that also likely to be so in Quentin's case?"

Barnabas stared down at the carpet in silence for a moment. Then he said, "There are things beyond our understanding, things that don't make sense in the usual fashion. And yet we know that they exist and there is a power associated with them. Until tonight you would not have believed in a potion that would bring a man two thousand years dead to life."

Her brow furrowed. "King Rehotip was not brought back to any kind of normal life. He is nothing but a wild phantom of the night now. There is no bond with humanity in him."

Barnabas nodded. "I know what you mean. I think this situation may be more dangerous for all of us than Anthony realizes."

"I agree," she said worriedly. "I wonder what he will tell the others."

"What suits him, if I know Anthony." Barnabas rose from the divan and picked up his silver-headed cane. "And now I must be on my way."

She strolled to the door with him. "I hate to see you leave." She was trembling a little. "This house has fresh terror for me now."

Barnabas patted her arm. "Be sure this door is locked and the others. It is not likely Rehotip will come back here in any case. He is more apt to wander aimlessly."

"Be careful yourself," she told him.

"You needn't worry about me." He kissed her goodnight and left.

She quickly closed the door and locked it, then hurried to her own room. Once inside it, she braced the chair against the door as she had other nights. Outside a mournful wind had begun to buffet the house on the cliffs. She could almost hear the murmuring of ghostly voices in it. And so she went over to the window and gazed out into the restless blackness.

At first she saw nothing. But as her eyes became accustomed to the dark she was able to make out the pattern of the surrounding grounds and the distant cliffs. It was then that she spotted the weird, solitary figure limping along the very edge of the cliffs. Her heart almost stopped at the sight of the linen wrappings trailing from the macabre creature the once proud King Rehotip had become. Lost in another age and another world, the mindless creature vanished in the shadows.

She drew back from the window with a feeling of nausea. What crime had Anthony Collins committed on this winter night? And how much guilt did she share as his companion in bringing that tormented soul into activity? Was the curse of Osiris to prove it had not lost its strength by causing destruction in a different way? She slept little that night, and when the gray morning came she was frightened and unhappy. For breakfast she was only able to manage a slice of toast and some coffee. The pretty maid, Bessie Miles, who had waited on her looked at her with troubled eyes.

"Aren't you feeling well, Miss Evans?"

She managed a weak smile for the girl. "I have a headache," she told her. "I had broken sleep last night."

"So did I," the girl said promptly. "My room is on the ground floor at the back of the house. And close to midnight I heard some strange screams."

"Oh?" Maggie knew it must have been the agonized cries of Rehotip the girl had heard.

"They were different from an ordinary scream," the maid said. "I can't think of words to explain them. But my blood fairly curdled and I couldn't get properly to sleep afterward."

"I know how you must feel."

The girl sighed. "Jack and Emma Radcliff are always teasing me with scary stories out in the kitchen. They do it to be funny, but the things they tell terrify me. They say there have often been vampires at Collinwood. You know—the walking dead who drain blood from others to keep their kind of half-life."

Maggie said, "I'll have Professor Collins speak to them. They shouldn't frighten you with such stories."

"I wish you would, Miss Evans," Bessie said gratefully. "But don't let on I complained."

"I'll see that the hint is dropped tactfully to them." After she left the breakfast table, Maggie tried to locate Professor Collins. She wanted to talk to him before the others returned. She had no idea when they would be back but she suspected it probably would be much later in the day. The professor was not in his office nor in the study so she decided to go down to the cellar, on the chance he had already begun work down there.

She found him in the large back room, kneeling beside the golden casket. And she was startled to see that there was a new mummified figure in it, tightly bound with the resinous linen wrappings of the original one. Anthony Collins glanced up at her as she hesitated in the doorway.

"Good morning, Miss Evans," he said in his dry way. "How do you like the new mummy of King Rehotip?"

"It looks almost exactly like the real one."

"I'm glad you think so," the Egyptologist said grimly. "It certainly wouldn't fool an expert. It's one I brought back on a previous expedition and have been keeping here for additional work. It came in very handy. With some luck we may prevent the others from knowing that Rehotip escaped us."

She stared at him. "You aren't going to tell them the truth?"

"Not yet." He scowled. "This will give us a little time. Professor Martin might spot the substitution if he looked at this figure closely. But we won't allow that. Neither Price nor Harriet Fennel know enough to catch on to what I've done. And I expect silence from you."

"I can only guarantee that if there are no bad results from that mad creature being loose."

Anthony Collins smiled bitterly. "You are emulating the noble Barnabas in that. His false front makes me sick. He doesn't fool me!"

She ignored this. "Are you going to pretend the coffin of the king wasn't opened?"

"That is my plan. The others won't return until this evening. I will replace the cover on the outer wooden box. We didn't split it in taking it off. I'm almost certain we can fool them."

"What about when they find out that mad creature is still at large?"

His stern face betrayed no emotion. "I'm sure Rehotip will have died long before anything like that happens. It is my belief he perished from the cold within minutes after leaving the house."

"I'm sorry to contradict you," she said with irony, "but after I went to my room last night I saw him making his way along the cliffs."

Anthony Collins lost his composure. "Are you sure?"

"Yes."

"Which way was he heading?"

"In the direction of Collinwood," she said. "He seemed to be limping."

The Egyptologist nodded. "That is as it should be. He was born with one leg shorter than the other. It is in all the history accounts."

"So he is not dead yet."

"He wasn't dead when you saw him last night," the professor corrected her in his cold fashion. "He must be by now. So I doubt that a search party is needed."

"I would feel better if there was one."

"You mustn't think of it at all," Anthony Collins said going over to his desk. "We will keep ourselves busy with other work and you'll be better able to drive such thoughts from your mind."

"I'll never forget the horror of his rising from the coffin."

Anthony wheeled on her, the pale blue eyes angry. "Don't talk about it!" he ordered. "I'm still unhappy that we confided in Barnabas last night. I don't think he can be trusted."

"I'm sure that he can be."

"You have so much trust in Barnabas," the old professor sneered. "What if he should also be proven a fugitive from the grave?"

"I still would have faith in him," she said firmly.

The stern face relented a trifle. "I didn't mean to anger you," he said placatingly. "I suppose Barnabas is an honorable man. But this is such a dread secret I hate to share it with anyone."

"If Rehotip threatens the countryside, you may have to share the truth with everyone."

He turned his back to her and in a low voice said, "Let us get down to work."

She assisted him in the dank gloom of the badly lighted cellar room until lunch time. Then she went upstairs with a feeling of escaping. Within a few days, as soon as the fate of the escaped Rehotip was settled, she would leave the red brick house. In the meantime she would try hard to adjust to its weird atmosphere and strange inhabitants.

The phone rang and Mrs. Radcliff came to tell her, "It's for you, Miss Evans."

Wondering who it might be, she went to the phone and cautiously said, "Yes?"

"It's David," came from the other end of the line in a familiar boyish voice. "How are you?"

"Very well, and you?"

"When are you coming to visit me again?"

"Soon," she said. "I had a rather unpleasant experience the other night on the way from Collinwood. But your father came along and drove me here."

"You were scared by a wild dog. He told me."

"Have you been out skiing?"

"You bet!" the boy said. "And I saw some ghost tracks in the back field this morning."

A chill shot through her. "Ghost tracks?"

"Yes," the boy said. "They went by Collinwood and the old house where Barnabas is living and then down the hill to the cemetery. I was skiing on that hill and I saw that the tracks went through the cemetery gates."

"You shouldn't be down there alone."

"But I was skiing," he protested. "I often ski on that hill. It has a good slope."

"Just the same, I don't like you way down there alone," she worried.

"Then come and ski with me."

"I may just do that."

"Would you?" the lonesome boy asked delightedly.

"Maybe."

"When?"

"I don't know. Whenever I can get some time off here."

"This afternoon?" David asked wistfully.

"I'll see," she said. "Why do you call the tracks in the snow ghost tracks?"

"Because they're funny," David said seriously. "They don't look like the marks left by ordinary shoes. They have a kind of odd shape."

She pictured the linen-wrapped figure of the disinterred king and felt ill. "Keep away from that cemetery."

"Why?"

"It could be dangerous."

David sounded interested. "You think it might be a ghost? It walked in around the graves. And I didn't go in there."

"Don't!" She spoke more sharply than she meant to.

There was a short silence at the other end of the line. "Are you mad at me?"

"Nothing like that," she said, trying to sound more cheerful. "It's just that I think cemeteries aren't proper places to ski."

"I guess not."

"So you keep away from that one."

"Sure," he said. "But Barnabas goes there a lot. And at night."

"What Barnabas does is of no concern of yours."

He ignored this, saying, "My father says that all the people who were friends of Barnabas are in the cemetery. That's why he goes there."

Maggie had a sinking feeling. But she pretended to accept these words casually. She said, "Your father says a lot of strange things. You aren't supposed to understand them all."

"Would you go to the cemetery at night?"

"No," she said. "I wouldn't even want to go there in the daytime. And don't you go either."

"Will you come over this afternoon and ski with me?"

"I'll see."

"Then I can show you the ghost tracks," he said. "Better come before there's another storm and they get covered up."

"I'll keep that in mind."

"And don't tell my father I called you."

"Why not?"

"He'll say I was bothering you. He doesn't like me using the phone. Not even to call him."

She laughed. "I won't tell your father."

"I'll be looking for you this afternoon," David said and then hung up. There was no doubt in Maggie's mind what the ghost tracks indicated. The picture of a demented and violent Rehotip trailing through the snowy fields to find sanctuary in the Collins family cemetery was vivid in her mind. What instinct had directed this tortured creature in linen grave wrappings to seek a hiding place in those snow-covered tombs?

CHAPTER 8

When Anthony Collins came up from the cellar she confronted him with the news she had heard from David over the phone. The stern old professor listened to her with growing concern.

"The tracks led into the Collins family cemetery," Maggie finished, "so that is where Rehotip is probably lurking now."

"I say he has gone there to die," the Egyptologist declared. "That is how the primitive instincts work."

"I'm not so sure," she said. "May I have the afternoon and evening off?"

His eyes narrowed. "Why?"

"The boy, David, has asked me to go skiing with him," she said. "And I'd like to see those tracks for myself. It's possible they could belong to someone else."

"Barnabas, for instance?" Anthony asked mockingly. "I hear he often prowls in the old cemetery."

She was blushing and angry at the same time. "May I have the time off?"

"Why not?" Anthony Collins said. "The others won't be back until late. And there's not much left for us to do here alone."

"Roger will drive me back."

"One thing," the Egyptologist warned her, a finger pointed at her. "You are to say nothing about Rehotip's escape to Roger at this time. I will let him know if there is any serious trouble. Otherwise I expect your silence."

"I remember our agreement," she said coolly. She had no idea what the fanatical Anthony Collins hoped to gain by keeping this information from Roger and the others. But she was sure he had some scheme in mind.

As soon as she finished lunch she dressed for skiing. Her skis were at Collinwood and she would pick them up when she met David there. It was good to escape from the bleak red brick house with its shadowed crates from the ancient dead world. The horror she had experienced beside that golden casket in the cellar would always haunt her. The distorted bronze face of the revived mummy had tormented her dreams the night before and would come to terrify her again many times in the future, she was sure.

She had also come to dislike Anthony Collins. She had no doubt that he was dedicated to his profession and an extremely clever man. He had also known many frustrations and disappointments, such as having the originals of those exquisitely jeweled golden scarabs taken from him by the Egyptian authorities. And so he had set great store on making himself famous by returning King Rehotip to life.

But now she felt he was being selfish in not informing the authorities, even though they might not take him seriously. And she also felt he was much too spiteful in regard to Barnabas. He had greatly resented taking Barnabas into their confidence and only the fact that he had appeared at the moment of crisis had made him agree to do so. Now he was doubly bitter in knowing he was at the mercy of the handsome British cousin.

Barnabas could reveal the truth about the escaped Rehotip any time he thought the danger of the situation warranted it. So Anthony Collins fumed and waited.

She began to hope that the tracks would prove to belong to someone else. Anthony Collins might be right; Rehotip might be dead and the danger over. She could only pray that this would be true. Meanwhile, the afternoon was cloudy and another snowstorm threatening. The tracks could be erased in a few hours. Now was the time to examine them and try to come to some conclusion.

Collinwood had never looked so inviting. She mounted the steps and rang the front door bell. The buxom Mrs. Stamers answered the door and her round face lit up with a smile when she saw Maggie.

"Master David will be glad to see you," she promised. "He's been waiting ever since lunch."

"I have to get my skis in the rear hall," she told the housekeeper.

"When will you be coming back to stay?" Mrs. Stamers asked as they walked down the hall to the rear of the mansion.

"I hope in a few days."

"That will be a relief," Mrs. Stamers sighed. "That boy doesn't mind me at all when you're not around. Not that I blame him since I'm sure he misses you."

Maggie smiled. "And I miss him."

She found her skis just at the time David came rushing out to join her, wearing a brilliant red stocking cap and his green ski outfit. His boyish face showed a broad smile. "I figured you'd come!"

"I told you I would," she said.

"A letter came from Aunt Elizabeth today," David said. "And she asked about you. And I had cards from Carolyn and Amy. Amy's wasn't much. I couldn't read all her writing."

Maggie laughed. "Well, at least she remembered you."

"Sure," he said. "Ready?"

"Yes. Where will we go first?"

"Out past the old house to the sloping field," David suggested. "That's so I can show you those ghost tracks."

"Oh, yes," she said with elaborate unconcern. "I remember you said something about them."

"You'll see!" he promised as they started out the back door.

When they reached the old house where Barnabas was staying, she felt a strong desire to stop in and talk to Barnabas. But she knew it would be no use. Barnabas never saw anyone during the daytime hours. That was why she had planned to remain at Collinwood for the evening meal. In that way she would be sure to see the man she loved. He would either stop by the big mansion as he did almost nightly or she would go see him in the old house.

David pointed to the shuttered windows of the old house. "It looks like it was still deserted."

"Barnabas and Hare are in there," she said.

"You don't see much of them until it's dark," the boy said. "That Hare is ugly. He's chased me away from the house more than once. I told him he couldn't do that because Dad owns it. But he just shook his fist at me and growled."

She smiled. "You mustn't mind him. He's a simple sort of man. And Barnabas has given him orders he's not to be bothered."

They passed the house and went on to the sloping field. It was covered with a heavy fall of even snow with only the marks of a few ski trails showing on it. Down at the bottom of the field the ancient family cemetery of Collinwood huddled. Its motley array of gravestones and tombs jutted out of the coating of snow. In the winter the cemetery looked entirely different. The snow covered all the neat grave mounds evenly, so only the granite stones protruded from the drifts.

David had his skis on and gracefully swung down the field a short distance ahead of her. Then he brought himself to a halt and turned to wave to her. "Over here," he shouted. "This is where the tracks are!"

She had just adjusted her own skis and now she followed him. When she came to a stop close beside him she clearly saw the trail where the snow had been trampled in a curious way.

"See?" David pointed.

Maggie studied the tracks as they led down toward the cemetery. They weaved to left and then to right as if the person who had made them had been in a kind of daze. Certainty grew in her that the creature they had revived in the cellar—King Rehotip—had made the tracks. Terror stabbed through her again.

But her voice was calm as she said, "Perhaps it was someone on snowshoes. They sometimes come down this way."

"The tracks don't look like snowshoes," David said dubiously.

She managed a smile for him, poised with her ski poles in hand. "Let's get on with our skiing."

"You bet!"

For an hour and a half they skied happily. During this period Maggie managed several times to get near enough to the gates of the cemetery to see that the tracks did go in there. However, she said nothing to David about this, even though he'd made mention of it earlier. She wanted to get him off the subject.

Finally it was time to return to Collinwood. It was nearly dark as they trudged back, tired and full of the contentment of an afternoon well spent. Maggie was trying to think how she might get back to the cemetery alone and see where those tracks went . . . and if the frozen body of Rehotip marked the end of them.

As they came abreast of the old house she saw a faint light streaking through one of the shuttered windows at the rear. She told David, "You go on to Collinwood and tell Mrs. Stamers I'll be staying for dinner. I'm going to take a few minutes to go in and see Barnabas."

The boy looked none too enthusiastic. "Can't I go in and see him, too?"

"Not now," she said. "I have some important things to talk to him about. You go on ahead."

"Okay," he said resigned and left her to continue on to Collinwood.

She stood there in the gathering dusk for a few minutes until he was out of sight. She very much doubted that Hare would allow her to see Barnabas yet, as the suave Britisher seldom ended his day's work before it was completely dark. But she could return to the cemetery on her own and investigate where those tracks led. If she really hurried, she could do so without a flashlight and be on her way to Collinwood before darkness finally settled. She had no wish to be caught within the confines of that isolated place of the dead in the night.

She put her skis by the steps of the old house and hurried back down over the snowy field toward the cemetery. This time she followed the weird tracks. In her mind's eye there was continually a vision of that tragic figure of the long dead king. Why had Anthony Collins insisted on giving the poor creature the antidote? He should have known that even if the potion worked, something less than human would emerge from that golden casket.

At the iron gates of the cemetery she realized the light was failing quicker than she had expected. Her heart began to pound with fear and excitement. But she could not give up yet. She must discover whether Rehotip was alive or dead. She strained to see where the tracks went as they weaved between the gravestones.

Mixed with her fear was annoyance at Anthony Collins. He had promised to make a search for the missing Rehotip that morning but had blithely forgotten about this or deliberately made up his mind not to organize any search. He had seemed more interested in covering up by installing a substitute mummy in the casket of the king. Perhaps he was counting too much on Rehotip perishing in the snow and was loath to let others know what he had done.

Now she was moving in the shadows of the gravestones. They tilted out of the heavy snow like dark sentinels. In the fading daylight they almost seemed lurkers skulking in the gloom. It was getting colder, the snow crunched under her feet. She strained to follow the tracks which continued their uneven path across the graveyard toward the forest beyond.

She followed around a tomb and then halted. Nothing broke the silence of the near darkness and yet a sixth sense had alerted her to some threatening danger. Her eyes searched the array of tombstones before her for some hint of movement from near them. But there was none. Neither had she found Rehotip's frozen body as Anthony Collins had predicted. And yet the tracks went on.

And then she heard a slight crunching of the snow. From around the corner of the tall tomb a brown, clawlike hand twisted and writhed like some obscene serpent, as if it were groping for something. She gave a scream of fear!

She had recognized the hand, it was Rehotip's. Seconds later the arm with its resinous tapes was revealed and then that grotesque wanderer from the past staggered into view. The cruel, brown face was still distorted with madness as the burning eyes focused on her. The thing that once had been ruler of the world's greatest empire came stumbling toward her, those revolting hands outstretched.

Maggie screamed again and turned to run, but she slipped in the snow and sprawled face downward on the ground. In the next instant she heard the labored panting above her and those steel hands gripped her and whisked her up as easily as if she were weightless. She kept on screaming, sure that she had betrayed herself to death this time.

Suddenly from behind her came a shout in a familiar voice.

"Maggie!" It was Barnabas.

Still holding her, the mummy emitted one of those piercing insane shrieks. At the same instant Barnabas reached them. And with a strength she had never suspected, he tore her from the arms of the graveyard horror.

She fell back against the cold granite of the tomb as Barnabas and the mad king met in an all-out struggle. Barnabas cried out some words in a tongue unknown to her and a surprising thing happened. The fugitive Rehotip staggered back, stood motionless for a bare moment and then turned and fled in the direction of the forest.

Barnabas quickly turned to her. "Did he harm you?"

She shook her head.

"You were foolish to venture in here after dark."

"I know that now," she said weakly. "I thought he had come here to die. Professor Collins was certain he'd perished from the cold."

Barnabas looked bitter. "Anthony has made more than one error." And he took another glance toward the forest to see if Rehotip was still in sight. He had vanished among the tall array of evergreens.

Maggie was staring at the profile of the man in the caped coat as he stood etched against the darkness. "What did you say to that creature? What made him suddenly cease struggling and run away?"

He turned to her again. "Some words in his native tongue. They seemed to reach him."

"How do you come to know his language?"

He smiled grimly. "Egypt was one of the countries included in my years of wandering."

"Is there anywhere you haven't been?"

"We'll talk about that another time," he told her. "Just now I want to get you out of here." He took a few steps in the snow and retrieved the silver-headed cane, which he'd dropped in the struggle. Then he grasped her by the arm and led her toward the cemetery gates.

She was weak and trembling from her ordeal and thankful for his support. "How did you know where I was?"

"Hare saw you place the skis by the steps," he said. "Why didn't you come to me first?"

"I didn't think Hare would allow me to see you."

"Darkness comes early these days," he said. "I would have gone down here on my own or at least gone with you."

"As long as you arrived in time."

"That was luck," he reminded her as they started up the steep incline of the snow-covered field. Ahead of them the old house was outlined against the darker sky.

"Where do you think that creature will go now?" Maggie asked fearfully.

"I can't guess. You mustn't try anything like this again."

"I realize that," she said. "Anthony Collins has to do something about reporting the facts to the police."

"Don't be surprised if he comes up with a good reason for not doing it."

"The others will be back from Boston tonight," Maggie said. "He's going to have a hard time keeping it from them."

"How long do you plan to remain there?"

She sighed. "I don't know. Not long. I would like to see this terrible situation cleared up before I leave."

"That could take a while," Barnabas said grimly.

"I'm having dinner at Collinwood," she told him. "Will you come along?"

"Not tonight."

"Why not?" She glanced up at him and saw that his handsome face wore a troubled expression.

"I don't think it would be wise," he said. "I have an idea Roger may not be in a good mood tonight."

She was surprised. "Why shouldn't he be?"

Barnabas gave her a bitter smile. "It's just a guess on my part. I'll see you safely to the door of Collinwood and then go on my way."

Maggie felt depressed. "I looked forward to spending some time with you."

"Another night. I may drop by Anthony Collins' house tomorrow night. As long as you're there I think I should keep an eye on you."

"You have," she said with gratitude. "What do you think will happen to that poor crazed creature?"

"I may go back and try to locate him after I leave you."

"Wouldn't that be dangerous?"

"I think not," he said carefully. "I have a deep feeling of sympathy for that lost soul. His madness cannot be blamed on him. And he is abroad only because of Anthony's greed for fame."

"I couldn't agree with you more," she said bitterly. They were close to Collinwood now. The lights at the windows of the great house reflected on the snow to make a cheery winter scene. Maggie wished that life at the estate was as calm and pleasant as it seemed. But now the dark shadow of the crazed King Rehotip threatened them all.

Barnabas halted at the steps. "Remember, no more foolish moves on your part."

She nodded. "You will keep in touch with me?"

"You know I will."

"And if you find Rehotip, let me know."

"I promise." And he took her in his arms and kissed her gently. "Go in now. And it might be wise not to mention me to Roger."

She was puzzled by his words, and the stiff formality of Roger's greeting when she entered the house. "Barnabas isn't with you, I see.

David said you were staying behind to pay him a visit at the old house."

"I did see him briefly."

At dinner David monopolized a good deal of the conversation. Roger sat quietly, even sullenly, at the head of the table. Once again Maggie had the impression that something was troubling him. But it was not until David went up to bed that he invited her into the luxuriously furnished living room and talked to her frankly.

When she was seated on a divan, he said, "This is a time when I wish Elizabeth was here."

"Is there any problem?"

"Yes." He gazed at her grimly.

"I'm sorry."

"So am I," he said. "And the worst part of it is that I don't know what to do."

"She'll soon be back."

"I know. But I'm not sure whether this problem will await her return. Last night a girl was attacked in the village."

She felt a surge of fear. "Oh?"

Roger's face was grim. "To make it worse, it was a girl from the plant. One of the secretaries in my office."

"What happened?"

"She was walking along a lonely stretch of road after visiting a friend and someone came out of the darkness and clasped a hand across her mouth so she couldn't scream. Then he gave her a savage kiss on the throat."

Maggie tried to keep calm. "Did she see who it was?"

"No."

She relaxed a little as she said, "That's unfortunate." Roger's eyes met hers. "Still, I'm sure I know who it was."

She frowned. "How can you?"

"By the girl's condition," he said. "There were two red marks on her throat. And she was in a dazed, weakened state when she stumbled into the front door of her house. Yet this morning she seemed quite herself again except for those telltale throat marks. I've known cases like this before."

"Here?"

"Yes," he said with a sigh. "And it was Cousin Barnabas who was blamed for the attacks in those other cases."

"And you're blaming him again?"

"Why not? This is the first attack since that other time. And Barnabas is back here again."

She demurred, "That isn't much evidence."

"I don't need much," Roger snapped. "Oh, I expected you to plead for him. But I warn you he's not to be trusted."

"I merely feel you should be sure," she protested.

"I'm as sure as I need to be," Roger worried. "The suspicion that Barnabas is a vampire has always been present. Once again I'd say he's proven it."

"I see," she said quietly.

Roger stood there stiffly with his hands behind him. "Did Barnabas mention this to you?"

She paused a moment before saying lamely, "He didn't want to come in."

"No wonder. He knew I'd tackle him about this. I've even considered calling Elizabeth long distance and asking her what I should do."

"You're being hasty."

"I don't think so," he replied. "When Barnabas was accused of the same things here before, Elizabeth asked him to vacate the old house. I should likely do the same thing."

"But your secretary didn't see who attacked her," she pointed out. "It could have been anyone."

He shook his head. "Not with those telltale marks on her neck and the strange feeling of dizziness she experienced. I call them Barnabas' trademarks."

"Then you've made up your mind."

"I'm afraid so," he admitted. "I want no scandal. But if Barnabas is going to slake his thirst for blood at the throats of young girls he'd better do it somewhere else."

Maggie stared at him unhappily. "How can you think such things of a man like Barnabas?"

"Because I believe he is tainted with the same curse as his ancestor. Elizabeth suspects the same thing. And so do many of the villagers."

"Suspicion and proof are two different things."

He frowned. "If only Barnabas would leave on his own. Since he knows that I'm aware of what happened, it would be the wise thing for him to do. But I fear he won't."

"And if he doesn't?"

"I can't let him remain here and expose us all to gossip and perhaps have him seized by the authorities. The Collins name is worth more than that."

"I doubt if things will get that bad."

"It will only need another attack or two," Roger predicted moodily. "And if Barnabas is truly a vampire, those attacks are bound to come."

"Since Mrs. Stoddard will be home so soon, you could probably wait to discuss this personally with her," she suggested, thinking this might give Barnabas more time.

"I'm not certain I dare wait."

"Worse things could happen here," she said, thinking of the mad

King Rehotip.

It was his turn to stare at her. "What do you mean by that?"

She knew she had spoken too freely. "I only meant there could be any kind of accident or disaster."

Roger was studying her suspiciously. "You sounded a lot more definite than that."

"I'm sorry. I didn't mean to."

"I understand you're a close friend of Barnabas," he said. "But I don't think you have any right to hold information back from me."

"I'm not," she said. And then confused and upset, she added, "Is it fair to be so sure that he is a vampire? There was a time when Quentin Collins suffered the same injustice from you here at Collinwood. Only in his case he was supposed to have the taint of the werewolf. Isn't all this kind of talk beneath contempt for modern, intelligent people?"

Roger regarded her coldly. "I consider myself a modern and intelligent man," he said. "But I have severe doubts about Quentin Collins. Either he became insane or he was suffering from some strange condition. At any rate he also left here under a cloud."

"But many people liked him!"

"Perhaps they were not aware of his character as we were," Roger said. "Admittedly, he could be charming. But when his seizures took hold of him he was sick mentally."

"Then he should have had treatment rather than be ostracized by his family," Maggie declared indignantly.

The blond man gave her a contemptuous smile. "There are conditions that modern medicine cannot touch."

"So now we slip back into the field of superstition once again."

"Are you trying to make things easier for Barnabas by pleading Quentin's case?"

She considered. "Perhaps so."

"It won't work," Roger said, "since I consider them both as tainted individuals. All the same I don't want us to quarrel about this."

"Nor do I," she said. "I suppose it is something you must settle with Barnabas directly."

"That is so."

She stood up. "It's getting late. I'd appreciate it if you'd drive me back to the red brick house."

"You've not decided to leave yet?"

Maggie smiled grimly. "Not yet." And then as they walked towards the hallway, she asked, "By the way, have you met Professor Herb Price, the young man who is assisting your cousin?"

"No," Roger said.

"It might be an interesting experience," she said with a thoughtful expression on her pretty face. "He'd probably remind you of someone you've known before."

CHAPTER 9

When Maggie left Roger's car and went to the front door of the red brick house it was Professor Herb Price who let her in, smiling warmly. "I wondered where you'd gone on this wintery night."

She returned his smile. "I was visiting Collinwood. Did you enjoy your stay in Boston?"

"Very much," he said. "But I'm glad to be back here. What did you and Professor Collins accomplish while we were gone?"

"A good deal, I'd say," she told him with an irony he could not understand. And then on an impulse she asked, "Did you ever meet a cousin of Professor Collins named Quentin?"

For a bare second the young professor looked startled. "Quentin Collins?"

"Yes."

"I've never heard of him," he said blandly. "But then I only met the professor when I came here."

"I keep forgetting," she said. "You were working in New York. I imagine you have many friends there."

He looked uneasy. "New York is not a city in which you make a great many intimate friends."

"But you would be known in your profession. Professor Herb Price would be a familiar name around the various museums."

The young man stared at her. "Why did you bring up the name

of this Quentin Collins?"

She pretended innocence. "I thought you might know him."

"Why?" he asked sharply. "Is he an Egyptologist?"

"No," she said. "But he probably spent some time in New York. And he is much your type. In fact, you resemble him to a large extent, except he doesn't wear glasses."

His eyes showed a cold light. "You interest me," he said softly. "I would like to meet this Quentin."

"I'm sure that you will."

"You're an unusual girl, Maggie," the young professor said. "I hardly know what to make of you."

She shrugged. "I'm a very plain person."

He smiled grimly. "I wouldn't say that. I find you subtle and much different from what you pretend. You are wasting your life working in this isolated village as a governess. You could take your place anywhere in the world. Be somebody!"

"I'm satisfied with my position," she said quietly. "Again I do not believe you."

She found the situation getting difficult. "Where is Professor Collins? Has he retired yet?"

"I believe not, though Professor Martin went directly to bed. He was exhausted. But I have an idea Professor Collins is in his office being briefed on the Boston trip by Harriet Fennel." He smiled wryly. "I waited here to meet you and all I got for my trouble was to have you compare me to some other man."

"Don't feel bad about it," she taunted him. "I believe Quentin Collins is a nice man, though he has had troubles. I'll go upstairs and see if I can locate the professor."

She left him and quickly went up the stairs. When she reached the second floor she could hear the voices of Harriet and Anthony Collins through the open door of his office. She moved slowly down the shadowed hallway and presented herself in the open doorway. The two halted in their conversation to stare at her questioningly. Maggie said, "May I speak to you a moment privately?"

Looking nervous, Anthony Collins got to his feet at once. "Of course," he said. "Miss Fennel is just leaving."

Harriet darted an angry glance at Maggie. Rising, she turned to the old man and said, "I'll tell you the rest of the details in the morning."

"Excellent," Anthony said brusquely, plainly anxious for her to leave.

She took her time about doing so, giving Maggie another arrogant look as she passed her. The moment the old man's secretary had vanished into the hallway he motioned Maggie inside and quickly closed the hall door to give them privacy. Then he looked at her with frightened eyes.

"Yes?" he said.

"I have bad news."

"What sort of bad news?"

"King Rehotip did not perish from the cold as you'd hoped. He is still very much alive. He was hiding in the old cemetery. Now he's taken refuge in the forest." Anthony Collins frowned. "I can't believe he'll survive long. It's not possible with the temperatures dropping to zero at night."

"Don't bank on it."

"At least he hasn't harmed anyone. So we've not caused any trouble by our policy of silence."

"Searchers should be out looking for him," she insisted. He was evasive. "I'll see what I can do."

"I only hope you don't leave it too late and so bring disgrace on yourself," she warned him.

Anger flared in the pale blue eyes and then disappeared. "I'll take care of the matter," he said in a mild voice.

She left his office feeling he would do nothing. "Remember," he said, stepping out into the dark hall with her, "You promised me your silence."

She gave him an annoyed look. "Only up to a point." She moved on to her own room, where she barricaded the door with a chair as she did every night now. And then she slowly began to prepare for bed. One of the last things she did was take a brief glance out the window. And she saw that snow had begun to fall. The storm had finally come.

Her thoughts at once went to Rehotip, hiding in the forest. What would happen to him now? And where could Barnabas have gone in this growing storm? One thing was certain, the snow would quickly cover the tracks of the insane king. She got into bed and turned out the lights. Roger had shocked her with the news that one of the village girls had been attacked and that he considered Barnabas the prime suspect. Then there was the mystery surrounding Professor Herb Price, who she was now convinced was Quentin in disguise, using this means to return to Collinwood. But why hadn't Anthony Collins become suspicious of him? For if this young man was Quentin, then he knew nothing about Egyptology and Anthony should have been easily able to spot him as an impostor.

It was very confusing. But more alarming than any of these other things was the knowledge that a violent lunatic had been set free to prey on the countryside by Anthony Collins. And she'd had a part in it. Unless the tormented creature that had once been a powerful king perished there was bound to be serious trouble. If Rehotip should attack or kill anyone, she would feel she bore part of the blame. Perhaps she should talk to Roger about this tomorrow and have him contact the proper authorities. It seemed the only solution that would set her mind at rest.

She would simply have to defy Professor Collins in this. He was so obsessed with his desire to gain fame for his findings in the Rehotip tomb that he cared about nothing else. His sense of fairness and judgment could not be relied on. She must make her decisions by her own standards of right and wrong.

She awoke later to stare up into the darkness with alarm on her pretty face. Outside in the hallway measured footsteps were coming in the direction of her door. She raised herself up to listen more intently. The footsteps brought to her mind the limping and mutilated ancient king in his linen wrappings. Her flesh crept and she waited.

The footsteps halted outside her door and then she heard the door handle turned. She held her breath. Pressure was exerted against the propped chair. But the chair held. And after a moment the attempt to force the door ended and the measured footsteps moved away.

She gasped with relief and lay back on her pillow. Who or what had it been?'And why had they wanted to get into her room? Then a shrill cry, somewhere between a wail and a scream, came from outdoors. It lasted only a minute but it made her quake with fear for a second time. After that there was a grim silence. And at last she again fell asleep.

She was at the breakfast table the next morning with the ancient Professor James Martin when Herb Price joined them. Martin was giving her an impromptu lecture on Egyptology which he didn't interrupt when Herb Price sat down at the table. He merely nodded to the younger man while Maggie and Herb exchanged amused glances.

"The greatest of the Pharaohs of ancient Egypt was Ramses," the old man told her. "The four figures of Ramses at the entrance of his temple rise 66 feet high and for over three thousand years have been miraculously protected against wind erosion by a sheltered location. The great temple is dedicated to the Lord-Ra-Horakhti, the rising sun, and the smaller temple of Nefertari, the royal wife, is dedicated to the Goddess Hathor. For years the area was the worshipping place of ancient Egypt. It receives the first rays of the sun in the early morning."

"Fascinating," she said.

"There's a good deal more," Professor Martin said, pleased. "I'll give you some books on the subject."

Herb Price gave her a mocking smile across the table. "You should visit Egypt one day, since you're so interested in it."

She said primly, "I'm sure you've been there many times."

"Of course," he said, and at once gave his attention to his plate.

She saw that she had made him nervous. Knowing that if he was Quentin he had never been to Egypt at all, she taunted him further by suggesting, "You should compare notes with Professor Martin."

Unwittingly the old scholar began to play her game. He gave

Herb Price a squinting look and said, "That's an excellent idea. We've never talked shop, Price."

"No," the young man said, without looking up.

"When were you last in Egypt?" Professor Martin wanted to know.

"Yes, do tell us," Maggie said, enjoying turning the tables on him.

Herb Price had actually gone pale. "I was there not long ago."

"Then you've seen the Aswan Dam of course?" the old man said.

"Of course," Herb said stiffly.

"There is a fascinating quarry there which you must know," Professor Martin said, his pinched old face eager as he warmed up to a favorite subject. "The Pharaohs of Ancient Thebes obtained pink granite for their temples from it. And discarded there is a huge wedge of stone cut for an obelisk, abandoned because of a crack that marred it."

Harriet Fennel came slowly into the dining room. It took Maggie a second or two to realize something was wrong. The secretary's attractive face was ashen and there was a look of horror in her eyes. She came nearer them before she spoke.

Then in a tremulous voice, she informed them, "There has been a dreadful tragedy."

Herb Price was on his feet at once. "What's happened?" he asked, going to her side.

Old Professor Martin struggled to his feet and turned to her. "Yes, what is it?"

Harriet swallowed hard. "A girl has been murdered."

Maggie was also on her feet. "What girl?"

Harriet looked at her blankly, all the arrogance drained from her. "Bessie. Bessie Miles, the lovely little maid."

"No!" Herb Price said sharply. "Who would want to do such a terrible thing?"

Harriet shook her head. "I can't imagine."

"When and where did it happen?" Professor Martin wanted to know.

"They found her this morning. On the beach. She was wearing only her maid's uniform and no outside winter clothing. It looks as if she went to answer the door and someone attacked her and dragged her outside without warning."

"How was she killed?" Maggie asked in a hushed voice.

She was almost sure the answer would involve the mad King Rehotip.

Harriet frowned. "I don't think they know exactly. The workman who found her body said it seemed she'd been pushed from the cliffs. The fall would have killed her."

"Perhaps she was running from someone and toppled over," Maggie said.

"But why would she go outside without warm clothes in the first place?" Harriet asked.

Professor Martin looked badly shaken. The old man's hands were trembling. "Where is Professor Collins?"

"He's getting in touch with the Chief of Police in Ellsworth," she said. "They look after Collinsport as well."

"I trust this doesn't upset our work here," the old man worried. "We have been making such great progress."

Herb Price gave him a reprimanding look. "A girl's life has been taken. I think that should be the gravest concern for all of us."

Surprisingly, Professor Martin's pinched face showed anger at this. He glared at Herb and told him, "The murder concerns only the life of one unimportant young female. The work we are engaged in is of the utmost importance to all the world. There is no comparison."

"There is for me," the young professor said with a tone of contempt. "I'm not lost in my work to that extent!"

"You don't understand!" Professor Martin complained as Herb strode out of the room. He turned to Harriet and Maggie with a pleading air. "I meant no harm. I have as much compassion as any man. I merely stated facts. Our work is important beyond any local murder and I wouldn't want to see it interrupted."

Maggie said quietly, "Your facts may be true but they would be better presented at some other time."

They all went out to the living room where the workman who had found the body sat uneasily on the edge of one of the divans, wearing his red and black plaid mackinaw and with his fur cap twirling restlessly in his hands.

Professor Martin advanced to him. "Where is the girl's body?"

"Still on the beach," the man said. "I got a blanket from my jeep to put over it."

"Have you any idea how long she might have been there?"

"Nope," the man said awkwardly. "But there was more than a little snow on her from the storm. So I'd say she must have been there most of the night."

"I suppose she could have stumbled over the cliff," Maggie suggested.

The man in the plaid mackinaw gave her an astonished look, "I don't rightly think so, miss. Not when you figure that Bessie lived in this village all her life. She was running along them cliffs when she was a little girl. It don't seem natural that she would fall off them as a grownup." Maggie said nothing more. She moved across the room, ignoring Harriet and Professor Martin who continued to question the workman. Maggie was remembering the pretty Bessie and her friendly ways and trying to think of what reason anyone might have for killing her. It had to have been an act of madness . . . in which case the fugitive King Rehotip was the most likely suspect.

At that moment Professor Collins came down the stairway from his second floor office to join them. She was at once struck by the way the senior professor had aged at the news of the murder. He looked a full ten years older than when she had last seen him the previous night.

He moved silently across the room to them with a stricken look on his stern, lined face. "The police are coming."

"How soon?" Harriet Fennel asked.

"They're on their way now," he said dejectedly. "It will mean a questioning of all of us and the usual investigation."

"But they know none of us in the house had any part in it," Professor Martin protested.

"I'm afraid we'll still be the first questioned," Anthony told him. "And we'll remain under suspicion until Bessie's killing is solved."

"Our work will be put back weeks," Professor Martin worried.

"That is an unfortunate possibility," the senior professor admitted. He glanced around. "Where is Professor Price?"

"I don't know," Harriet said. "He left the dining room ahead of the rest of us."

The workman, still seated on the divan and looking extremely uncomfortable, spoke up. "If you mean the young fella with the horn-rimmed glasses, I think he went to the cellar."

Anthony Collins nodded approvingly. "He's probably going to try and get his work wound up before the police come. We might all be wise to follow his example."

Harriet nodded. "I'll go down and assemble the cards we'd made out before going to Boston."

"And I have some notes I wanted typed," Professor Martin said in his querulous old man's way. "This is most unfortunate." He and Harriet Fennel moved on to the cellar door to vanish down the rickety steps.

Anthony Collins told Maggie, "You wait a moment, Miss Evans. I have something to say to you."

"Very well," she said quietly.

The professor dismissed the workman politely. "Thank you for what you've done. I think you should go back and wait with the girl's body until the police arrive."

The man jumped up from the divan with relief. "Yes, sir," he said with an energetic nod. And he put on his cap and let himself out the front door.

There was a long moment of silence in the sun filled room before Anthony moved over to Maggie again. In a troubled voice, he said, "This is a horrible business. Jack and Emma Radcliff are sitting out in the kitchen in a state of shock. They were very fond of the girl."

"We all were," Maggie said brokenly.

He frowned and looked down at the hardwood floor. "Yes, I fully agree. I wouldn't be surprised if we lost them as help. And I don't know who we can get to replace them. This affair could be disastrous to our project."

She gave him an angry look, annoyed at the lack of true feeling in him. "Can't you blame yourself a good deal for what happened?"

He stared at her in surprise. "Why?"

"It was you who revived King Rehotip and allowed him to escape. And knowing he was a madman you still said nothing and wouldn't permit me to tell anyone but Barnabas."

"So?"

"It's plain enough that he came back here and hurled that poor girl over the cliffs to her death."

His eyes narrowed. "You're going to tell the police about Rehotip and blame him for this crime?"

"Who else can be blamed? If you don't tell them I certainly will."

"You'll be making a mistake," he warned her. "They need not know about him yet."

"I say they should and must," she said defiantly.

There was a strange look on his stern old face. "There is something about Bessie Miles' death you don't know. I have been down to the beach with the workman and Jack Radclilf and seen the body. So I know what I'm talking about."

"What do you mean?"

His pale blue eyes held that gleam of madness again. "I examined the body closely and I found two red marks on her throat."

"Two red marks," she echoed faintly.

"And you know what that means," he said with malicious triumph. "Not Rehotip but Barnabas! It is Barnabas who leaves red marks on the throats he drains of blood!"

"I don't believe you!"

"You'd be wise if you did," he warned her. "One mention of Rehotip to the police and I'll draw their attention to those marks. Unless I do so they aren't liable to notice them and Barnabas won't be suspected. But if I point the marks out your friend Barnabas is as good as in jail.'"

"You're blackmailing me."

"If you want to put it that way," he said calmly. "Or you can look at it from a more sensible viewpoint and see that I am protecting Barnabas and also our work here."

"Always your work!" Maggie said with disgust.

"It is important to me and the others associated with me," Anthony Collins said sternly. "I cannot expect an outsider like yourself to have the same feelings."

"Bessie is dead!" she told him. "I have feelings about that. And I don't want that mad creature killing others!"

"It probably wasn't Rehotip," the professor argued. "But all I'm asking for is time. Give me that and I promise to be fair. If indications point to Rehotip being the murderer I'll reveal the full facts to the police. But I don't want to do so needlessly. And by that I mean if Barnabas or some local person was the murderer."

"You know it wasn't Barnabas!"

"I'm sorry," he said. "But I'm ready to blame him before anyone else. Consider for a moment. Suppose he merely seized her and stole blood from her throat, leaving her in a dazed state. He might have then fled into the storm. He would assume she'd gone back into the house. But instead she may have stumbled towards the cliffs in her semi-conscious condition and fallen to her death. He needn't have intended her to die or pushed her to her death. But his need for blood was the cause of her death indirectly."

On the verge of hysteria, she raised her hands to her ears. "I don't want to hear any more."

He came over and roughly grasped her arm. "I won't discuss it then. But I will count on you to say nothing for the moment."

"I don't know," she said, her eyes blurred with tears.

"I'm afraid you have no choice," he told her, "unless you want to tie your close friend Barnabas to a murder."

"I don't believe anything you've said," she protested. "How do I know there are such marks on that girl's throat?"

"I'd advise you to take my word for it," he said. "I wouldn't bluff in such a serious matter. I'm not trying to conceal a crime. But we are engaged in a most important project here and I must try and protect it every way I can. If some of my means seem cruel and twisted, I regret it. But above all I am dedicated to my career."

She said, "And if the clues lead to Rehotip?"

"I will tell the police the entire truth and take all blame for your remaining silent," he promised. "I can't do more than that. Now I suggest you go to your room and try to compose yourself until the police from Ellsworth get here."

Grateful for a chance to get away from him, Maggie started toward the stairs. But she'd only gone a few steps before he halted her by speaking to her again.

"There is one other condition to my protecting Barnabas. You must remain here as long as I need you. I'll require your services more urgently than ever after this setback and help will not be easy to recruit."

"I'll think about it," she said quietly.

"I suggest that you think very seriously about it."

In the privacy of her room she stood before the window facing the cliffs. She was still stunned by the news of Bessie's murder. She stared at the landscape with its fresh white coat of snow, glistening in the December morning sunshine and the silver of the ocean beyond. It was hard to believe that somewhere down on that beach the body of Bessie was stretched out rigid and frozen.

Professor Collins had revealed himself as the fanatic she'd always felt him to be. His findings in Egyptology meant more to him than anything else. And it was true of Professor Martin as well. She had seen a different redaction in Harriet, and Herb Price had been as badly shaken by the tragedy as Maggie herself. And if he were Quentin Collins? His real identity should soon come out, once the police began their investigations.

She was worried most about Barnabas. Anthony Collins had cruelly suggested the man she loved was a vampire and that he had killed Bessie for her blood, either directly or indirectly. This, combined with her knowledge of the earlier attack on the secretary at the fishing plant and Roger's certainty that Barnabas had been responsible, made a strong case against the handsome Britisher.

But opposed to all this circumstantial evidence, and it was only circumstantial evidence, was her belief in Barnabas. She wasn't sure what problems he faced but she believed him to be a decent person; not a murderer.

She didn't expect her convictions to count much if the senior professor deliberately placed Barnabas in the spot of chief suspect by stressing those marks he claimed were on Bessie's throat. Marks that could even come about as the result of the fall.

Could she take the chance of defying Anthony Collins? She feared not. She had barely reached this conclusion when she heard her name called by Anthony Collins from the head of the stairs. She went out and saw him standing waiting there for her with a troubled expression on his lined face.

"The police want to question you," he said in a low voice. "They're waiting below."

"Very well."

He still blocked her way. "Remember what I told you."

"I know," she said wearily.

"In any case, I'd say they know who the murderer is."

She gave him a frightened look. "Who?"

His pale blue eyes met hers. "Professor Price," he said. "He seems to have disappeared. There's been no sign of him since Harriet announced Bessie's murder."

CHAPTER 10

A week had passed since the discovery of Bessie Miles' body on the beach. It had been a week of strange tensions and startling developments, the most puzzling of which was the disappearance of Professor Herb Price. The police search for him had been extended to surrounding states, as it was generally assumed that he was involved in Bessie's death.

Maggie, convinced that Herb Price had been Quentin Collins in disguise, had other theories. Knowing that as soon as the police came he was in danger of being found out, he'd had no choice but to vanish. In her opinion he had not been connected with the maid's death in any way.

It was a Tuesday night and below-zero weather along with strong winds had returned to the Maine coast. Maggie stared through the living room windows at the road leading to Collinwood, considering making a visit there to talk with Roger. David had phoned her many times and had complained of things being dull at the big mansion. There had been no mention of Barnabas; she badly wanted to talk to him. But she didn't like to ask Roger to come for her with the car and she didn't dare hazard walking up there alone.

Her reverie was broken by the sound of footsteps behind her and she turned to see Professor Anthony Collins had entered the room, a troubled expression on his lined face. He looked weary and older.

"I have had further word from the police concerning Herb Price," he said.

"What did they have to say?"

"There's no record of him in New York at all," the old professor said bitterly. "He has never been registered in the state. In other words, he was an impostor."

"I'm not surprised."

He frowned. "The police seem to question my judgment in hiring him without making more inquiries. The thing they seem to miss is the desperate urgency I had to get the cataloging of the Rehotip collection started, and my lack of competent help. At the time I hired him, Price seemed a windfall to me."

"He managed to bluff along very well."

Anthony Collins made an impatient gesture. "He was doing only subordinate work on a level not much higher than the type you engaged in since you came here. And I admit he talked Egyptology well. He'd probably done a lot of reading on the subject."

Maggie smiled ruefully. "The Curse of Osiris is being headlined in the papers again. Did you see today's Boston Globe? They have a feature story linking your work with that of the first expedition. And they describe all the mysterious deaths associated with the first expedition, connecting them with Bessie's murder and Professor Price's disappearance."

"Cheap sensationalism!" the professor said angrily. "I suppose we'll have to put up with a good deal of it until this blows over."

"People are superstitious. And history does seem to be repeating itself. I wonder how they would handle the true story if they knew it? What they would write about a revived and mad Rehotip roaming the countryside?"

The pale blue eyes of the professor fixed on her coldly. "If you have any thoughts of making a statement to the press, remember that Barnabas is not in the clear even though the spotlight of suspicion is on Herb Price. I want your continued silence." He turned to stare out the window at the dark, cold night. "In any case it's all hypothetical. Rehotip is surely frozen to death by this time."

She gave him a reproving look. "You said that before, but it wasn't true."

"A long time has passed since then."

"I'm still doubtful."

Looking angry, he said sharply, "It would be much better if you didn't give this any thought at all. The important thing is to carry on with our work here as if nothing had happened."

"That's rather difficult," she said. "I'd like to visit Collinwood for a change. But I'm afraid to go up there and back on foot."

Anthony Collins became more genial. "Why didn't you mention it before? I'll give you the keys to the station wagon. You can drive up and back."

"I didn't want to bother you."

"It's no bother. Despite our differences, there's no need for you to feel yourself a prisoner here. How can you properly work with that attitude?" And he reached in his jacket pocket and passed the keys to her. "Feel free to use the station wagon whenever you like."

In her gratitude she almost forgave him for the way he had blackmailed her into silence. After all, he was fanatically devoted to his work and felt anything was ethical that would help push it forward.

She held the keys and said, "I may go up for a short while this evening."

"Whenever you like," he said with a wave of his hand.

"I imagine Elizabeth will be returning in about ten days. She and the girls expected to be back in time for Christmas. She'll want me to return to the house then."

Anthony Collins sighed. "If we are not held back further I'd expect to have all the important work done within ten days. In any case, you can leave when she returns."

Maggie heard this with elation. She had been afraid that he might continue his blackmail to make her remain at the red brick house indefinitely. "I only spoke of it because Roger might question me."

"Of course." Then, in a somewhat crafty manner, he added, "Perhaps you may see Barnabas when you're at Collinwood."

She was at once on guard. It was what she'd hoped but she didn't want him to know. "That's doubtful."

"He'll no doubt be relieved that the police are looking for our bogus professor," Anthony Collins said pointedly.

Maggie excused herself saying she wanted to leave for Collinwood before it got too late. She went up to her room and began putting on her winter wraps. While she was doing this she heard a gentle knock at her door.

With a slight frown she went over and opened it to discover Harriet Fennel standing there. For once the attractive dark girl had an uncertain look. All the old arrogance in her bearing seemed to have vanished.

"May I speak to you a moment?" she asked.

Maggie hesitated, not wanting to be abrupt, but eager to be on her way. "I'm dressed to go to Collinwood," she said. "But I don't mind talking for a few minutes." And she opened up her coat.

"I wanted to talk to you about Herb Price. Do you really think he was an impostor?"

"According to what Professor Collins says, he was."

"But you knew him. Didn't you find him pleasant?" Harriet persisted.

"He was very nice."

"I don't believe he killed that girl," Harriet Fennel said. "I don't care whether he was an Egyptologist or not. I don't think he is a murderer."

"You may very well be right," Maggie assured her, feeling the same way.

Harriet looked worried. "I don't understand Professor Collins' attitude in this. But then there are many things here that puzzle me."

"We'll probably hear from Herb Price again."

"I hope so. I've never been superstitious but I'm beginning to put some stock in the curse associated with Rehotip's treasure. Lately I've been hearing things in the night. I believe this house is haunted by the ghost of that ancient king."

"We've been subjected to a great deal of strain," Maggie said. "It's no wonder you're upset."

Harriet gave her a look of gratitude. "Thank you for giving me this time," she said. "I appreciate it. Perhaps we can talk again later."

"Of course."

"There are some other things troubling me," Harriet said. "And I'd like to have your opinion about them." Maggie saw her out and then went quickly downstairs and outdoors. The night was terribly cold and it took her a few minutes to get the car going properly. Frost showed on all the windows and she turned on the defrosters to full strength as she drove off. She began to think Anthony Collins was right. Rehotip could never survive in weather like this.

She had been interested in what Harriet had to say. And she guessed that the dark girl had really been very fond of the young professor. Would she care about him the same way if she knew he was Quentin Collins and bore the werewolf curse?

It took only a short time to reach Collinwood in the station wagon. David came to the door to greet her and she spent a short time with him until he went up to bed. Then she sat and chatted with Roger before the log fire in the softly lighted living room.

Roger was in a subdued mood. "I enjoy it in here on these zero nights," he said. "I'm glad you drove up. It was a good idea of Anthony to let you have the wagon. I've been planning to stop by and see you but every night there has been something."

"Things have been tense down there since Bessie's death," she said. "The police have been around continually and the professor complains about losing working time."

He studied her speculatively. "Do you think it might have been an accident? That the poor girl fell over the cliffs without anyone else being involved?"

"I doubt it," she said slowly. "Though I suppose one shouldn't rule out any possibility."

"The question is, where has Herb Price gone? It's my idea he's hiding away not far from here. And why should he do a thing like that?"

"There could be many reasons besides the possibility he is a murderer."

"Yes. But isn't that likely his strong motive?"

"I haven't decided," she hedged.

Roger emptied his pipe in an ashtray on the table by his armchair. His eyes were still on her. "You must have some theories. The Boston Globe in its story today seems ready to put it down to the ghost of Rehotip being at work again."

She smiled grimly. "I read that."

His almost handsome face showed interest. "Is it true there are three unopened coffins in the cellar of the house? And the corpse of the king is in one of them."

"There are three coffins," she said carefully.

"I hardly think I'd enjoy Anthony's profession," Roger said in a dry voice. "Spending your days in dusty tombs searching for the dead and their belongings doesn't appeal to me."

"He thinks of it in a different sense. The benefits such revelations bring mankind. It's the best way of finding out about the past."

"I suppose there is that aspect of it."

She had not mentioned Barnabas to him and neither had he spoken of his British cousin. But when the front door bell of the old mansion rang shortly after nine she felt a thrill of expectation. It was just possible this would be Barnabas, she thought. And she sat nervously waiting for Roger to answer the door and return.

And then she heard Barnabas and Roger exchange greetings. She could tell Roger was extremely restrained and she heard Barnabas inquire about her. Roger told him where she was and a moment later the two men appeared.

It was the first time Maggie had seen Barnabas since the murder of the maid. He came directly to her and said, "I'm sorry I've neglected you in the past few days. But I've been away."

She smiled up at him. "I was sure something was wrong."

He frowned. "I was distressed to hear about Bessie. She was a nice girl."

"We've all been shocked."

From the fireplace where he was standing, Roger spoke up sharply. "You can be grateful for the crime in a way, Barnabas. The furor it's caused and the spotlight being on the missing Herb Price has made people forget about you. Your name isn't being mentioned at all."

"I had no idea," Barnabas said with a sober look on his gaunt face.

"It might have been wiser for you to have left Collinwood rather than merely go away for a few days," Roger warned him.

"You think so?" Barnabas asked with a touch of irony in his resonant voice.

"I'm positive of it," Roger said. "I'm going up to bed now. I'll let Maggie reason with you. She's your good friend and I'm certain she'll tell you the same thing." He gave her a look of bitter amusement. "Give him your best advice, Maggie." And with a nod he marched out of the door.

Barnabas waited for him to go upstairs before he took Maggie in his arms for a lasting kiss. Then he looked at her with a troubled gleam in those deep-set eyes. "I'm afraid things are becoming more complicated."

"I've been so worried about you."

"I know," he agreed with a sigh. "But usually I attract the wrong kind of attention. People regard me as an eccentric because of my way of living and dress. I hesitated to show myself much at the home of Anthony Collins with the police nosing around."

"I understand what you mean," she said. "You know all about Herb Price vanishing."

"For the same reason," Barnabas told her grimly. "There's no question that he is Quentin Collins. And he can't stand police investigation either. I'd say he was a long way from Maine by now."

"Some think he may be hiding near the house."

"Because they don't understand the situation and that he is Quentin," Barnabas said. "I have no doubt that my idea is the correct one."

She gave him a worried look. "I suppose you've been wondering if it was Rehotip who killed Bessie?"

"I've taken that for granted," he said. "Why hasn't Anthony reported his being loose to the police?"

She made a wry face. "He has some crazy reason for not wanting to. And he bound me to silence by threatening to involve you."

Barnabas looked startled. "How did he manage that?" She hardly knew how to tell him. In a strained voice, she said, "He mentioned the rumors about you in the village. That you'd attacked young women there and telltale red marks had been left on their throats. And he claimed there was the same kind of mark on Bessie's throat."

"What if there were?" Barnabas demanded. "That needn't mean that I had thrown her over the cliffs. And the chances are there likely weren't any marks on her throat at all. He bluffed you."

"I couldn't take a chance," she faltered. "I couldn't risk getting you involved."

His manner became gentler. "I understand that, but I'm afraid Cousin Anthony has taken advantage of you. He's a wily fellow."

"When it comes to protecting the Rehotip treasure, I'm sure he'd do anything."

"It was undoubtedly that mad creature who hurled Bessie to her death. Why won't Anthony admit that? If he told the police they could send out a proper search party to find Rehotip."

"He won't listen to reason."

"We must find a way to change that," Barnabas said with a grim note in his voice. "At least you have the station wagon to get you safely home. You'd better start before it is too late."

"When will I see you again?"

"I'll call by the house shortly," he promised. "No need to worry about the police now. They've probably completed their investigation and it will be safe for me to show myself again."

"I've missed you so."

"And I've missed you."

He escorted her out into the cold night and saw her safely into the station wagon, promising to keep in touch with her. He was standing there, hatless, as usual, as she drove away from Collinwood in the winter night. Snow covered the fields and even remained lightly on the road. Roger had the plow leave a coating for traction. The great elms surrounding the old mansion had been mantled with white and the air fairly snapped with frost.

She drove fairly fast, anxious not to spend time alone on the road. Fear still haunted her. The knowledge that the insane fugitive from the tomb was still at large filled her with stark terror. Her headlights wavered up and down as she headed along the rough private road. With some relief she saw the red brick building in the beam of the headlights and a moment later brought the station wagon to a halt beside the other car in the parking lot.

Turning off the ignition, she was about to extract the key when she heard a rustling in the station wagon behind her. Very slowly she let her eyes turn to the right to glance over her shoulder. And she saw the withered brown hand! It reached out over the back of the seat and was about to take hold of her!

Screaming, she flung the door wide and jumped from the station wagon. Then she ran to the rear door of the red brick house and threw it open. A frightened Jack and Emma Radcliff stood together in the kitchen staring at her.

The handyman came to her. "What is it, Miss Maggie?"

She gasped, "Out there! In the station wagon! A hand appeared over the back seat!" She didn't explain that it was the hand of Rehotip.

Jack Radcliff held back, obviously reluctant to mix up in trouble of any sort. "I'll call Professor Collins."

She remained in the warm kitchen with her teeth chattering from sheer fright. Visions of that bronze, distorted face and the near-frozen mutilated body tormented her." Somehow the insane creature had found the station wagon and taken refuge in it from the cold. And she had driven all that distance without knowing the horror that had been so near her!

Anthony Collins, looking shaken, appeared with Jack Radcliff. "What's this about the station wagon?"

"Out there!" she said. "I saw a brown hand reaching over the back of the seat. It tried to grasp me!"

He stared at her. "That's a strange story!"

"Believe me!"

He gave her a warning look to say no more. "Jack and I will go out and have a look." Then he and the handyman left by the back door.

Emma Radcliff gave Maggie a despairing glance. "I knew we should have left here after what happened to Bessie. It's the curse! Everyone knows about it. It was in the Boston paper today."

"Wait until they come back," Maggie said, a tremor in her voice.

In a few minutes the two men returned. Anthony Collins had put on no hat or coat and now he stamped the snow from his shoes. He looked chilled to the bone as he gave her an odd glance. "There was no one in the back of the station wagon."

"There had to be!"

"No sign of anyone," he said grimly. "Jack will back me up in that."

The handyman looked unhappy. "That's right, Miss Evans. There wasn't a sign of anyone in the back of the wagon."

"He had plenty of time to get away," she said, feeling cheated and afraid.

"I suggest you go to bed," Anthony Collins said. "You're overwrought."

She nodded without making any further protest. What point was there in it? But as she mounted the stairs to the second floor she remained convinced that it was Rehotip who'd threatened her.

Her night was restless, and when morning came she was filled with misgivings about the silence concerning the fugitive Rehotip she'd pledged to Anthony Collins. If Barnabas was right, the senior professor was merely taking advantage of her. The chances were there had never been red marks on the throat of Bessie at all.

She went downstairs and had breakfast alone. When she returned to the living room she met Professor Martin. The bent old scholar seemed troubled.

"I'm looking for Miss Fennel," he said. "Have you seen her?"

"No."

"She's not in her room. I was sure she'd be down here, but she isn't."

"Could she have gone ahead to the cellar?" Maggie suggested. "She may have wanted to get an early start."

"I don't think so," he frowned. "She never goes down there without one of us with her. And there's little she could do alone. She's not in the dining room?"

"No," Maggie said. "I've just come from there."

A new idea seemed to come to the old man's mind. "Perhaps she is in Anthony's office. I didn't think of that before. I'll try up there."

"Do you want me to go for you and save you the steps?" she asked. "I'm going to my room for a moment anyway."

His pinched old face showed appreciation. "That would be kind of you," he said. "I'll wait here."

She quickly went upstairs and to the closed door of Anthony Collins' office. She knocked; he invited her to open the door and come in. She found him alone, seated at his desk.

He glanced up at her. "Yes? What is it?"

"Professor Martin is looking for Miss Fennel. He thought she must be here with you."

"She isn't. I haven't seen her this morning."

"I'll tell him," she said, and started out again.

He halted her by calling after her, "Just a moment. Miss Evans."

"Yes?" She turned to see that he was on his feet now.

He came toward her. "About last night. I'm afraid you're allowing your nerves to get the best of you."

"I did see a hand," she maintained. "It could only have been King Rehotip's."

"Impossible! The station wagon was empty."

"It was a long time before you went out there. He'd escaped by then."

Anthony Collins smiled coldly. "You don't give up an idea without a struggle, do you?"

"I know what I saw."

The professor shrugged. "I won't make an issue of it, Miss Evans. But I am worried about you. I'd better go down and see what is bothering Professor Martin. He becomes more childish every day!"

They went down the stairway together. She could tell he was annoyed. And she was beginning to wonder about Harriet. The dark girl had been in a strange mood the previous night, badly upset about Herb Price leaving. Could she have decided to leave as well, and without any warning? It didn't seem likely. She'd been the loyal assistant to Anthony Collins too long to do a thing of that sort.

Professor James Martin was waiting at the foot of the stairs expectantly. "Did you find Miss Fennel?"

Maggie said, "No. She wasn't with Professor Collins."

"Then where is she?" the ancient professor asked with shrill annoyance. "She promised we would begin a new listing together early this morning."

"We'll have to find that out," Anthony Collins said, a slight hint of uneasiness in his manner. Maggie volunteered, "I think she may have gone downstairs on her own."

"It's a possibility," Anthony Collins said. He glanced at his older colleague. "Have you been to the cellar yet?"

"No," the old man snapped. "I always wait for her."

Anthony looked uncertain. Then he said, "We'll be going to the cellar in any case. So we'll see if she's there." He snapped on the stairway lights and started down the rickety steps to the earthen cellar floor. Professor Martin followed him closely, with Maggie in the rear. When she heard the strangled cry of Anthony Collins she couldn't tell what was wrong.

"What is it?" she asked.

Professor Martin seemed to have frozen on the steps. He pointed a thin finger. "See!"

Anthony was kneeling on the cellar floor before the sprawled body of Harriet Fennel. She pressed the back of her hand to her mouth to strangle the scream that hovered on her lips.

Anthony got to his feet and stared up at them sadly. "She's dead. She broke her neck in the fall!"

Professor James Martin moved slowly down to stand beside the body. "I can't believe it," he said shakily.

Maggie had descended to the next to the last of the wooden steps. Mercifully, Harriet's face was turned so she could not see it in death. She stared dully at the body of the girl she'd talked with only the previous night. "How?" she murmured.

Anthony Collins' lined face was distorted with grief. "She must have tripped and fallen."

"No!" Maggie said in angry protest. "There has to be more to it than that."

"You don't think it was an accident?"

"No!" she shook her head. "Someone hurled her down those steps!"

It was the aged Professor Martin who came up behind her and made an announcement that sent despair surging through her. The old man's quaking voice seemed barely in control as he said, "Very odd! There are two red marks on her throat, only a small distance apart."

CHAPTER 11

The hours following the discovery of Harriet's body were among the worst Maggie had ever known. Once again the police were called in to investigate the accident and once again she kept silent, fearing harm might come to Barnabas if she told about Rehotip being at large. But, after a routine investigation the police decided that Harriet had stumbled on the steps and her death was due to a normal accident.

Of course Maggie was convinced that the creature they'd revived from the golden casket was responsible. Yet that didn't explain the red marks on the girl's throat. This time she had seen them herself. She had forced herself to look at Harriet's shapely white neck before the police arrived, trying to ignore the expression of horror on the dead girl's face and her staring eyes.

But that frightened face and those eyes would not be erased from her mind. They seemed to be etched there. And long after Harriet's body had been taken to the undertaking parlors in the village and prepared for shipment to her home town in Ohio, the terror on that pretty face haunted her.

Professor Collins was lost without his secretary; it was several days before he was able to organize the work again. Now he counted on Maggie to do the more complicated work Harriet had been responsible for and frail Professor Martin was attempting to carry a double work load. It meant they all spent longer hours in the dungeonlike cellar.

During the days following Harriet's death there was no sign of Barnabas. Once again he seemed to disappear. Maggie went up to Collinwood twice, but neither time did she meet him. And the police had not been able to track down Professor Herb Price. The impostor seemed to have vanished into thin air. In a way Maggie was glad, because she didn't believe he'd had anything to do with Bessie's murder. Still Anthony Collins clung to the theory that the young man was guilty and was lurking somewhere in the area.

One evening in late December Maggie presented herself in Professor Collins' office. He looked up from his desk with a slight frown and said, "Yes?"

"I wanted to ask you about leaving on Monday," she said. "I expect Elizabeth will arrive home that afternoon."

The professor looked unhappy. "But surely she won't need you her first day back?"

Maggie stood there determinedly. "I'd like to be at Collinwood to greet her."

"You can be, but that doesn't mean you'll have to give up your work here."

"I want to."

"I'm afraid that's not convenient," he said coldly. "I still need your help. We're very far behind because of all that has happened."

"You promised I could leave when I liked."

He smiled icily. "When I said that, I didn't expect the developments we've had—one of our party dead, the police looking for another, and Professor Martin ready to collapse at any moment. I can't spare your services yet." "

I'll leave anyway," she said simply.

"I wouldn't want to have to talk to the police about the red marks we found on the throats of both girls," he said slyly. "They might jump to a lot of wrong conclusions and decide Barnabas was to blame."

"Haven't you used that over my head long enough?" she asked plaintively.

"I don't think so."

"Someone else could have made those marks to throw suspicion on Barnabas."

The professor studied her with those mad pale blue eyes. "I could tell the police that. They might be interested in your idea."

"No!" She didn't want him to mention Barnabas to the police at all. Not yet.

Anthony Collins shrugged. "Then let us leave things as they are. You give me your cooperation and I'll assure you of mine."

She made no reply. In a way, she'd not expected any consideration from him. He cared about nothing but the contents of those ghostly crates stolen from King Rehotip's tomb.

He pointed angrily to the open newspaper on his desk. "All the papers are picking up that curse story now. Harriet's accidental death has the story being repeated. I'm being plagued by reporters on the phone and some of them are bound to be showing up here. How can I convince them there is no curse of Osiris?"

"Perhaps there is," she said grimly, "and we're all victims of it. I feel like one. And who knows what may happen next?"

"Nothing will happen!" he said with annoyance. "At least it needn't. You're mimicking the newspapers when you indulge in such negative talk!"

"I try to face facts," she said. "Two mysterious deaths and an unexplained disappearance! No wonder the newspapers think it sensational, on top of the long list of violent deaths among the members of the first expedition."

"Ridiculous superstition! I would expect something better from you."

"And that poor unfortunate mad creature still at large?" she said. "What will happen when they find out about him?"

"They'll never find out. He'll die and that will end it."

"You've hoped that from the beginning," she reminded him. "But it hasn't turned out that way."

"It will," he promised. And then he rummaged on his desk and picked up a group of filing cards. "Will you take these down to Professor Martin? He's working alone in the cellar tonight."

"Very well," she said. "Then I'm taking the station wagon to Collinwood."

"Don't be too late returning. And watch out for Rehotip. We don't want him showing up in the back seat again."

She frowned as she took the filing cards. "There was something in that back seat."

"Of course!" Anthony Collins said blandly. "But all I know is that I didn't see anyone. It was empty."

With a sigh Maggie left him. He had a controlling hand over her and he was gloating in his power. If only Barnabas wasn't so open to a scandalous attack she'd leave at once. But. . . .

She went down the rickety cellar steps cautiously and once again had doubts that Harriet could ever have tripped and fallen to her death. She had been thrown down, probably by Rehotip. The first cellar room was deserted and so were the others until she came to the fourth and largest room where she and Anthony Collins had watched the mad king come alive.

In the fourth room Professor Martin was on his knees beside the coffin nearest the desk. He had the cover of the wooden box already open and was copying material from the bronze-like covering of the inner casket. This was by no means as elaborate in design as the golden casket in which the king had rested.

Maggie went over and held up the cards for him to see. "Dr. Collins sent you these," she said and placed them on the table.

He gave her a nod of thanks. "Kind of you. I'm copying the burial notes from this casket. It has plenty of talk about the curse included. Meant to frighten off the gullible, of course."

Maggie stood there in the murky light of the gloomy room and gave a small bitter laugh. "Perhaps I should be counted among the gullible then."

The old man raised his white eyebrows and stared at her with concern. "You're frightened?"

"Yes."

He sighed, still on his knees by the coffin. "I can't say that I blame you. All this is foreign to you. It is different for Professor Collins and myself. An everyday routine."

"Surely you can't consider the deaths we've had here routine?"

He looked troubled. "Yes. That's been unfortunate. Most unfortunate."

"I'm ready to think the curse is at work."

The old man raised a protesting hand. "You mustn't let the newspapers sway you with their nonsense any more than I am swayed by the warnings I'm copying from this casket. I know they were put there for a purpose and have no real danger for me."

"I wish I could feel the same way," she said. "But I can't."

"I'll agree there have been some rather mysterious incidents here I don't understand," the old man said with a frown. "But I feel in due time they will be explained."

"I haven't your patience."

"You're not working tonight?"

"No. I want to talk to Roger Collins. His sister is expected home soon and I'm anxious to get the details."

The old professor nodded. "Of course. Your interest is there with the children as mine is here with these relics. That is the way it is in life. We all must have our different patterns."

She felt rather sorry for the old man and managed a goodnight smile for him. "I wouldn't work too hard if I were you."

"This work must be finished soon," was his reply as he resumed his copying from the bronze casket.

Maggie never sat at the wheel of the station wagon that she didn't glance apprehensively behind her to see if there was any sign of an intruder lurking in the shadows of the rear seat. Her experience that night on the drive back from Collinwood had left her jumpy. But she was determined to get away from the red brick house for a little and that meant using the big car.

She'd been kept later than usual because of her long talks with both Anthony Collins and the old professor in the cellar. As she drove up the icy road to the great mansion on the hill she saw that there were only one or two faint lights showing from its windows. She began to worry that Roger might have gone to bed early as he sometimes did on these winter nights.

It was Mrs. Stamers who opened the door. The stout woman regarded her with surprise, "You're late, Miss Evans."

"Yes," she said. "Is Mr. Collins still up?"

"He isn't at home, miss," the housekeeper said apologetically. "And Master David has been in bed this half hour."

"I see," she said, hesitating on the steps. "Have you any idea when Mr. Collins will return?"

"Not until late," the housekeeper said. "He's working at the plant. It's getting near the end of the year and he spoke of having to close the books."

"Of course."

"You're welcome to come in and wait."

"I don't think so," she said, still standing there in the cold of the steps. "Has Mr. Barnabas been by lately?"

"No," the old woman said. "Not since the night you were here."

"But he's still staying at the old house, isn't he?"

"I expect so, miss," Mrs. Stamers said. "I heard Master David say he saw that Hare this morning."

"Thank you," Maggie said. "I'll come back again." Thoroughly chilled, she returned to the station wagon. For a moment she thought about going on to the old house and trying to find Barnabas there. But something told her Barnabas wouldn't be at home. He was much more likely to be out somewhere. And since it was Roger Collins she particularly hoped to talk to, she decided to drive into the village and see him in the office at the fishpacking plant. She felt sure he wouldn't mind her coming by for a moment.

There had been no fresh snow for a few days and now the roads had become icy. The lights of Collinsport were welcome. And she drove cautiously down the steep incline of the main street with the buildings of the plant owned by the Collins family showing straight ahead on the wharf.

Part way down the hill she saw the red and blue neon sign of the Blue Whale Tavern on her left. Barnabas sometimes frequented the place; perhaps he might even be in there now. She decided to take a gamble on this. Finding a parking place for the station wagon, she got out and carefully picked her way across the slippery surface of the street.

The jukebox of the Blue Whale was playing at blast level and the air was hot and filled with the fumes of tobacco smoke and alcohol as she entered the long, narrow building. As usual it was crowded. Some of the young men lounging against the bar gave her an interested glance as she moved quickly by them.

She went to the end of the bar and asked the attendant there, "Has Barnabas Collins been in here tonight?"

The man jerked his head. "He's in here now. In the booth at the back. You a friend of his?"

"Yes."

The bartender chuckled. "That's something. I didn't think he had any friends. There's a guy who's always alone!"

She made no attempt to answer this but turned and went down the long array of booths to the very rear of the building. And there alone in a booth sat Barnabas with a glass of beer on the table in front of him. Seeing her, he got to his feet at once.

Maggie went up to him and said reproachfully, "I've had a hard time finding you."

"Sorry," he said. "I've had things to do."

"Such as?"

"It's a long story." He indicated the empty seat opposite him. "Sit down." She did and he resumed his seat studying her with concerned eyes. He told her, "You look pale and weary."

"No wonder," she said with a bitter smile. "I happen to be both. Why have you avoided me?"

"It seemed the best thing to do," he said with a frown. "I didn't know what minute I might have trouble with the police. And I didn't want you involved."

"You've heard about Harriet's accident?"

"Yes."

"Only it wasn't an accident," she said unhappily. "I'm sure it was murder and that mad Rehotip was responsible."

"It could be," Barnabas agreed. "I've spent a lot of my time tracking your mad king down. Contrary to what Anthony claimed, he's still very much alive."

"I knew it," she said.

"A lot of his time is spent at the old cemetery."

"So he's gone back there."

"There's a tool shed in the far corner of the cemetery, away from the graves," Barnabas told her. "Much of the time he's been hiding in there. He seems to be afraid of the daylight. But after night he leaves the wooden shed and roams about widely."

Her eyes were wide with fear. "What is going to happen?"

"He should be put to rest."

"I agree," she said. "And I would tell the police if Anthony didn't threaten to turn them on you. He's blaming you for the deaths of those two girls." She paused. "There were red marks on Harriet's throat. It's not hearsay. I saw them."

The gaunt handsome face of the man she loved was grim. "I ask you to believe one thing," he said. "If there were marks on her throat they were not of my making."

"Of course I believe it," she said. "But would the police?"

"Probably not."

"So Anthony has full control of the situation," she said in despair.

"Perhaps not for long," Barnabas said. "Things will have to change."

"I hope so, and for the better," she worried. "I'm beginning to believe all those awful stories about the curse."

"Just take care that it doesn't reach out to you."

"Twice it almost has."

"In a moment you should leave here," Barnabas said. "I don't want our being together attracting attention. It could make trouble for you if anything happened."

"I'm not afraid."

"I am," he said firmly. "Where are you going now?"

"To the plant to see Roger Collins."

"Then start at once," he said. "It's getting late. And be very careful."

She started to get up, her troubled eyes on him. "When will I see you again?"

"I'll stop by the red brick house tomorrow night," he said.

"Do you mean it?"

His deep set eyes met hers. "I promise. Now be on your way."

She left him with a feeling of disappointment. She knew he had insisted on her leaving alone for her own good, but she would have preferred to have remained with him. The curious eyes of the tavern's motley group of patrons were fixed on her again as she walked out. She drew a deep breath when she stepped out into the fresh, cold air of the street.

She returned to the station wagon. Making sure there was no one in the back, she continued her drive down to the wharf. Since the wharf was wide she drove out on it to park the vehicle. The icy, black waters of the bay lapped around the wharf. She could hear the waves as she got out and walked towards the main offices of the fish plant. She saw lights at two of the windows, which meant Roger was there.

The door wasn't locked so she went right in and up a short flight of stairs to the office. The building smelled of fish and oilskins. She found Roger seated in his swivel chair busy at an adding machine. He swung around to greet her with a look of surprise. "I didn't expect to see you here."

"I wanted to talk to you. Mrs. Stamers said you were working."

He got up from his chair and came over to the counter to be near her. "Anything wrong at the house?"

"Nothing more than you know," she said with a sigh. "Now

Anthony Collins is making noises about not wanting to let me leave when Elizabeth returns on Monday."

"But he has to. He promised."

"He's singing a different tune now."

Roger looked annoyed. "We'll soon end that song."

"I don't want any arguments with him," she said hastily.

Roger stared at her in surprise. "You sound as if you were afraid of him."

She didn't dare tell him about the threat to Barnabas, so she contented herself by saying, "I think I am. Afraid of him and all the atmosphere of that gloomy old house."

"When the time comes I'll drive down and get you. Just put your bags in the car and let him try to make any complaints," Roger said. "I'll handle that gentleman."

Maggie smiled wistfully. "You give me courage."

"I was the one who suggested you go down there, but I didn't think it would turn out as it has."

"I know," she said. "Just so long as you understand."

"I'll come for you Sunday," he promised. "Have your bags ready."

"You can depend on that."

He looked at his wristwatch and frowned. "It's getting late. I'll soon have to leave. How are you getting back?"

"I have the station wagon."

"Good," he said. "Then you'll be all right. Just drive carefully. The roads are in bad shape tonight."

"I know."

When she stepped out on the wharf she felt nervous. The lapping of the waves in the darkness was an eerie sound. Hurrying across to the station wagon, she hastily started it and backed up to turn and head toward the main street again. In her hurry she neglected to check the rear seat. She had gone part way up the main street before she remembered. But when she made the check the rear seat was comfortingly empty.

Because of the icy road conditions there were few cars out. It was also getting late. She took her time and when she reached the red brick house on the cliffs it was almost midnight. A frosty midnight. She parked the station wagon and carefully locked it. As she was taking the key from the lock she had the sudden sensation of someone watching her. Someone close behind her.

Slowly she turned around, all her panic coming back in a surge, and saw the angry distorted face and mad eyes of King Rehotip staring at her. But his clawlike hands reached out toward her with more than a hint of menace.

Maggie screamed and backed away as the horror limped towards her. The thing opened its withered lips and made that shrill, shrieking cry again. She wheeled around and fled to the rear door, reaching it ahead of the pursuing monster. The door was unlocked. She frantically darted inside, slamming the door and locking it after her. Then she ran to the living room.

Anthony Collins was standing in the middle of the room. She ran up to him and cried, "Rehotip! He's outside. He chased me to the rear door. In a moment he would have caught up with me."

"You're telling me you saw Rehotip just now?"

"Out there!" she said, pointing dramatically.

"I find that hard to believe," the professor said. "I heard nothing until after your car pulled up a few minutes ago. Then you screamed just before you came in here."

"I saw him!" she said, horror in her voice.

"I'll take a look," Anthony Collins said coolly.

"Don't go out there alone," she warned.

He gave her an odd look. "I'll see what I can from the rear windows."

She went with him. They moved from window to window, peering out into the darkness and seeing nothing. The mad king had vanished.

She gave the Egyptologist a despairing glance. "I tell you he was out there."

His expression was disdainful. "I'd be quicker to believe you if I'd seen him."

"Wait and you will!"

"I'll come back a little later," he said. "Right now I want to see what's doing with Professor Martin. He hasn't come up from the cellar yet."

She stared at him with frightened eyes. "You mean he's still working down there at this hour?"

"He was copying an especially interesting inscription from one of the caskets," the professor said. "I expect he's lost track of the time,"

Maggie shook her head. "I'm worried. I think something must have happened to him."

Anthony looked annoyed. "You seem to be seeing trouble at every turn."

"There must be something wrong!"

"We'll soon settle that," he said grimly and stalked off in the direction of the cellar door.

She followed him with a sinking sensation. She had the feeling that she was about to witness another ghastly sight. The premonition was reinforced by her knowledge that the insane Rehotip had been lurking around the house, had perhaps even been in the house! The cellar!

They went down the rickety steps and through the dimly lighted rooms with their phantom packing crates and somber relics. At last they came to the large room in the rear where she'd seen the old professor at work earlier. A gasp escaped her lips as she saw his emaciated form slumped over the bronze casket.

Anthony quickly bent down and turned the body over. When he'd made a hasty examination he turned to her and said, "He's dead. Apparently a heart attack. Not surprising, the way he's been overworking."

"The curse!" she murmured.

He frowned, still kneeling. "None of that hysterical nonsense."

"It was Rehotip! He came down here and did it! I'm sure!"

Anthony looked disgusted. "I can't accept that!"

"Are you sure there are no signs of violence?" she asked, moving nearer.

"Not that I've seen." He turned to make a further check on the body. After a moment he gave a soft exclamation.

"What is it?" she demanded.

He looked at her again. "I didn't notice at first, but there are those same red marks on his throat as I found on those of the girls. Two marks a short distance apart!"

She frowned. "They can't have had anything to do with his death."

"Why not?" Anthony Collins asked coldly, rising to his feet and facing her. "Barnabas may have been here tonight."

"No!" she said. "I saw him in the village at the Blue Whale. If anyone made those marks, it had to be Rehotip!"

For the first time Anthony Collins seemed to be taking her seriously. She could tell that the death of his associate had hit him hard. He was studying her with those pale blue eyes. "You honestly think that Rehotip may have come down here and frightened Martin so that he had a heart attack and died?"

"Yes. I think those marks you've seen on the throats of those who have died here are of no importance. They happened to be there from one circumstance or another. But they have had no bearing on the way they died!"

"Perhaps you're right," Anthony Collins said slowly. "If so, that would absolve Barnabas of any blame."

"I've tried to tell you that from the first!"

There was a second of silence as they stood facing each other in the murky light of the cellar with the dead man beside them. Anthony Collins then gave her a wise look.

He said, "You've forgotten there is one other suspect who could have come back down here and scared Martin to death. The man who very likely murdered Bessie, and maybe Harriet as well. You know who I'm talking about; he's probably more dangerous than poor mad Rehotip. I mean Herb Price!"

CHAPTER 12

For the moment Maggie had forgotten all about the young professor, or rather Quentin Collins, as she knew him to be. She was startled to hear his name brought up now, when there was no indication he was within a thousand miles of Collinsport. But then, it really wasn't all that strange. Anthony knew him to be an impostor, without knowing the reason why. And she saw no need at this point to inform him.

Instead she shook her head and said, "Rehotip!"

Anthony Collins swallowed hard. "I suppose you're right. The police agree that Price is hundreds of miles away from here by now."

"So it has to be that madman."

"I hate to tell the police," he fretted. "They'll destroy him. Probably shoot him down. We'll never have a chance to find out if he could make a recovery—even a partial recovery. Think of the wealth of history he could tell us!"

Maggie looked at the old man sternly. "You have sacrificed three lives to preserving the small fragment of what was once a powerful king. Rehotip is nothing more than a rotting hulk of avenging flesh. It is right that he should die. All these weeks he's known a kind of twilight life that must have been torture."

"You state your case strongly." The old professor glanced toward his dead associate. "I guess you are right. The time has come for me to be frank with the authorities."

"It's overdue."

"They won't believe me," he warned her. "Outsiders will say Martin died of a heart attack, Harriet of a fall and Bessie was murdered by Herb Price. When I tell them of a mad king roaming the area, they'll think I'm insane."

"I'll back you in the story."

"They won't want to believe either one of us," Anthony Collins said grimly. "And if we do prove it, think of the field day the papers will have. All the business of the curse will be revived. I'll become a freak and no one will take the magnificent discoveries I've made in the Rehotip tomb seriously. My career of a lifetime will be ruined."

"It's that or risk more lives," she said quietly. "Have you any choice?"

The old Egyptologist glanced at the sprawled body of his dead friend again. "No," he admitted. "It seems that I haven't. But at least let us not give the story to the police until the morning. Otherwise we'll have reporters flocking in on us in the middle of the night."

She listened to his serious words and decided this was a fair enough compromise. The authorities needn't know that they had discovered James Martin's body before going to bed. It could just as well be in the morning. "Very well," she said.

They left the cold body of the elderly professor where it was, hunched by the bronze casket, and in a subdued mood went upstairs. As they reached the upper hallway Anthony Collins gave her a troubled look.

"I have a confession to make," he said with a deep sigh. "After what has happened to my old friend Martin, I'm willing to believe in the Curse of Osiris. There must be something in it."

She shrugged. "Earlier tonight he disavowed any belief in the curse. He said it had been devised merely to frighten off vandals."

"And now he is dead."

They went on upstairs to their rooms. But Maggie enjoyed little sleep as she tossed and turned through hours of fear. The memory of the figure of horror she'd seen in the yard of the red brick house was still fresh in her mind. Those brown, dried-up hands reached out to seize her in the few snatches of nightmare-filled sleep she managed. And when morning came she felt a deep sense of relief. At last it would be settled.

As she dressed she did a lot of serious thinking. It was most important that Rehotip be captured or eliminated with as little fuss as possible. It would be better for everyone this way, including the wretched mad king. And it seemed to her the man most suited to the direction of this operation would be Barnabas Collins. But Barnabas would never consent to breaking the usual routine of remaining in the old house until dusk. So if she were going to solicit his aid, she would have to wait until then.

More specifically, the police would have to wait until then. She decided to say nothing about the shed in the cemetery where Barnabas said Rehotip had been hiding. If the police found it on their own, well enough. If they didn't, she would suggest at dusk that the aid of Barnabas Collins should be sought.

She had breakfast alone. Tea and toast were all she could manage. Before she finished her tea Anthony Collins came in. He said, "I've been to the cellar again. And I've told Jack and Emma Radcliff of Professor Martin's death as if I'd discovered it just now. I've also put a call through to the police at Ellsworth."

"They'll be here soon then."

*"Yes." He sounded grim. "I still don't know whether I have the courage to go through with this."

"You must."

He sighed. "I know."

"The legend of the curse may help them to understand," she said. "They'll be prepared for something out of the ordinary."

"There will be the difficult question of why I didn't tell them before," he reminded her.

"You can say that until I saw Rehotip in the yard here last night, you were sure that he'd perished."

"That's still far from a satisfactory explanation."

"I'm afraid there just isn't one," Maggie said.

Two hours later she sat in the living room with an agitated Anthony Collins and a thoroughly shocked police inspector from Ellsworth. They sat in the divan in the middle of the big room while the tall, bluff man in plain clothes paced back and forth before them. He finally halted in his nervous pacing to give them another incredulous stare. "This is the craziest story I've ever heard."

"I'm afraid it's the truth," Anthony Collins said.

The inspector was grim. "I've read all this stuff about the curse and thought maybe there was something in it. Those fellows in the old days were close to nature and knew a lot maybe we don't even guess. So maybe anything is possible. Like poison left for intruders in the tomb. Or some kind of trap to kill them. But when you start telling me you and this girl revived a man who died more than two thousand years ago I find it tough to swallow."

Maggie explained, "We expected that. And that's why we've waited so long to tell you."

The inspector was indignant. "Much too long, as far as I'm concerned. Especially if as you say"—he took out his notebook to repeat verbatim what Anthony had told him—"Rehotip is violently insane in his reincarnation and is a threat to anyone he encounters." The inspector closed the notebook and glared at Professor Collins. "According to your own admission, he's been roaming the area for weeks."

"I'm afraid so," the professor murmured, staring down at the floor.

The inspector shook his head. "From the beginning I haven't liked what is going on here. But I didn't believe it could add up to anything like this."

Anthony Collins looked up at him. "I've told you the truth."

"A truth that I'll have to do some thinking about," the inspector warned them.

"It would be helpful if you would keep this information secret until Rehotip is captured," Professor Collins said. "If the press gets word of it the whole business could turn into a mad carnival."

The inspector looked indignant. "It's mad enough as it is. And how long do you think I can manage to keep this secret if I tell my men we're looking for a fugitive madman born two thousand years ago! A king at that! Do you have any idea what a tip like that would be worth to the Boston papers? My men are dependable but there's a limit!"

Maggie suggested, "Can't you merely say that you're looking for an insane man?".

Anthony Collins nodded. "That would be the best plan. When he is captured it will be time enough for them to know the whole truth. I can't impress on you how important it is to bring Rehotip in alive. I'm pinning great hopes on his regaining his sanity and being able to tell us something of his era."

"From all you've said that doesn't sound likely," the inspector said.

"Even a small hope," the professor replied weakly.

The inspector turned to her. "You were the last one to see him, miss?"

"Yes. In the yard outside. Last night, I was terrified." The inspector nodded. "But he got away before the professor could do anything."

"There was no sign of him when we searched for him later."

The inspector was watching her intently. "What kind of shape would you say he was in?"

"He looked dreadful. More of the tapes had been torn from his body. But I suspect he is still very powerful."

The inspector stared at them both glumly. "I hope for your own sakes that you're not putting me on! If so, I warn you it will be a serious business."

Anthony Collins rose with great dignity. "Do I strike you as the kind of man who would play a childish prank?"

The inspector hesitated. "No. But it is a wild story."

"It's the truth." Maggie also stood up.

The inspector sighed. "I'll send out an alert. Bring extra men into the area and tell them we're searching for a madman. That's as far as I'll go at the minute. I hate to think what the Chief will say when I show him my notes. I'll be lucky if he doesn't have me locked up for observation."

"We'll back you in this, Inspector," Professor Collins ' promised.

"You'd better. Have you any idea where we should begin our search? You know the places this king of yours has been seen."

There was a pause. Then Anthony Collins said, "Anywhere on the estate. I doubt if he's wandered away from Collinwood."

By afternoon several carloads of police had arrived and the search for Rehotip began. Maggie waited anxiously, almost certain they would have no success. And in a way this was the way she wanted it to go. She still had certain feelings about the treatment and rights of this unfortunate soul they had revived from the grave. And she knew that Barnabas would be more considerate of the fugitive than the police. He would also be much more likely to locate Rehotip.

Dusk arrived and there was still no word from the inspector. A few minutes after six an official police car drew up before the door and a moment later the inspector presented himself. As Maggie showed him into the living room, the big man seemed completely let down.

"We've been all over the estate and there's no sign of that fellow," he told them.

"You can't give up now, Inspector," Anthony Collins protested.

He gave him a sharp look. "I don't know about that. As far as I'm concerned a man died here of a heart attack last night. That's no police case."

"There were the other deaths," Maggie reminded him.

The Inspector turned his frigid gaze on her. "Harriet Fennel died from an accidental fall. That's what is in the books. And as for poor Bessie Miles, we know who killed her. And we're still on the lookout for your missing professor."

"Herb Price wasn't responsible," Maggie protested. "Rehotip had to be the one involved in all those deaths."

"I don't even know this mad king exists."

"He does, I assure you," Anthony Collins said.

Maggie decided the time had come to introduce Barnabas into the problem. "I know someone I'm sure can help us, even lead us to Rehotip."

The inspector raised his eyebrows. "You do?"

"Yes. It's Barnabas Collins, a British member of the family visiting in the old house. He's made a study of the supernatural and I'm certain he'll be willing to assist us."

The inspector turned to Professor Collins. "You know this Barnabas?"

The professor nodded grimly. "He is a student of the supernatural, as Miss Evans claims—in fact, to such an extent that the villagers have shown suspicion of him. There's a chance he could aid us." The admission came with reluctance. It was plain he still disliked Barnabas.

The inspector turned to Maggie. "Where do we find this Barnabas?"

"He's very retiring," Maggie said. "It would be best if I approached him on this alone. He's in the old house a distance past Collinwood. If you'll drive me there I'll talk to him."

"Let's go," he said curtly.

The inspector drove them over in the official police car. A spell of milder weather had set in, bringing with it a nasty drizzle and a curtain of land fog. It gave the night an eerie touch. The headlights barely penetrated the gray barrier in many places and they had to slow down.

As they passed Collinwood Maggie wondered what Roger was thinking of all the sudden police activity on the estate. She was sure he would be annoyed and hoped that it would soon be settled. Then, as they neared the old house, she began to have further qualms. Suppose Barnabas wasn't there? Or that he wouldn't agree to help?

The car came to a sliding halt on the slippery wet ice of the back road, the headlights reflecting ghostly patterns in the shifting fog. The inspector turned to her in the semidarkness of the car with the motor still running and said, "I'll give you five minutes, miss."

"I'll see what I can do," she promised.

Beside her Anthony Collins murmured, "Don't expect too much from Barnabas."

Feeling a small panic, she left the car and made her way across the treacherous surface of the road to the steps of the old house. Not a light was showing. She knocked and waited. After a moment she heard footsteps approaching and when the door opened it was Barnabas.

He looked surprised at seeing her and then glanced at the police car. "What's going on?"

"I need your help."

"Come in."

She entered the shadowed hallway and he closed the door to give them privacy. Taking her by the arms, he said, "You're trembling!"

She nodded. "Yes. Anthony has finally told the police about Rehotip. They want to capture him. I didn't tell them about the shed because I felt you were the one to direct this. You'll know how to manage it. I've already sold the inspector on the idea."

Barnabas hesitated. "I'd rather not have any part of it," he said at last.

"We can't allow that lost soul to remain at large," she said with deep sincerity. "Not for the public's sake nor for his. Anthony should never have brought him back to life."

"That goes without saying," Barnabas agreed. He sighed. "Very well. I'll lead the search party."

It was an hour before everything was organized and the police surrounded the old cemetery. Lanterns and strong flashlights gave the mist-shrouded night a weird glow. As the small party led by the inspector and Barnabas entered the cemetery and quietly approached the old shed, the tension reached the breaking point. Maggie and Anthony Collins were in the rear of the group along with an irate Roger.

"Why am I the last to be told these things?" he kept complaining. "A lunatic on the grounds and no one bothering to inform me!"

Barnabas and the inspector were only a dozen feet from the battered tool shed now. The tall man in the caped coat turned and gave the inspector a nod to indicate he believed Rehotip was in the shed. On this signal the inspector moved forward. He shouted for Rehotip to come out. Of course there was no response.

Then he rushed forward with his red-shaded lantern held high and threw open the door of the shed. For a moment it seemed that the tumbledown shack was empty. But as Maggie watched she thought she saw a stir in the shadows and a moment afterward the inspector cried out again and entered the shed.

A high-pitched maddened shriek cut through the air! And before the horrified eyes of the onlookers, the inspector and the creature in tattered linen wrappings locked in a struggle. The lantern was thrown to the floor of the shed in the battle and exploded into a glaring fire. The red flames showed the life and death struggle between the inspector and the inhuman figure of the king. For a moment Maggie could see the clawlike hands grip the inspector by the throat. Then Barnabas rushed into the flame filled shed. She screamed in alarm.

Seconds later Barnabas came back out, carrying the inspector limp in his arms. Behind him the flames were consuming the tool shed, sending greedy yellow tongues up through its roof and throwing a cloud of smoke to mix with the fog shrouding the cemetery. From the shed there came another long piercing scream and then the shack collapsed in blazing ruins.

Maggie ran forward to where Barnabas was kneeling by the prostrate body of the inspector. He looked up and in reply to her unasked question, said, "He's going to be all right."

Anthony Collins had also come forward and was staring at the burning ruins. "Lost," he said sadly. "Rehotip will never tell us his story! Lost to the world forever!"

Maggie looked at the troubled face of the Egyptologist. "Isn't it better this way? There was no hope for him."

"Perhaps," he said. But she knew he didn't believe it. Barnabas returned to the red brick house with her. Roger also came along. The inspector had recovered enough to be driven to the Ellsworth hospital in his own car. And he and Anthony Collins had come to a private arrangement not to reveal the identity of the man who had died in the shed. The inspector felt the story was too fantastic and Anthony was relieved at the prospect of avoiding further unwanted publicity.

As far as the public ever learned, it was a demented itinerant who had died in the shed, a dangerous madman who had wandered onto the estate of Collinwood.

The atmosphere in the living room of the old brick house was subdued. Emma Radcliff had made them coffee. Roger and Anthony Collins talked quietly at one end of the big room while Barnabas and Maggie were together near the stairway.

"I'll be leaving here tomorrow," she said with relief. "I can't stand it any longer."

Barnabas frowned. "Why not leave tonight?"

"I have my clothes to gather up and pack," she reminded him. "It will be easier to do it in the morning. Anyway, the danger is over."

Barnabas' deep-set eyes held a strange gleam. "I suppose so," he agreed. "It was very generous of Anthony to suddenly end his feud with me."

"He had to," she said. "He needed your help."

"He's said no more about the red marks on the throats of the three who died here?"

"No. He's certainly stopped trying to blame them on you," Maggie said. "And in thinking it over, I'm sure they weren't worth noting. Marks such as that could come about in a fall or through chafing."

Barnabas smiled thinly. "Yet on such slender evidence the legend of a vampire sometimes begins."

"Isn't it dreadful," she said with a tiny shiver. And she gave him a gentle smile. "At least you don't have to worry about that any more."

Roger came toward them and said, "I'm going home. Can I give you a lift, Barnabas?"

"Thank you." Barnabas turned to her. "I'll see you at Collinwood tomorrow evening."

"Yes," she said, glad that it was all over.

When the two men had gone, Anthony Collins said goodnight to her and she went upstairs to her own room. She was so thoroughly exhausted and relaxed that she hurriedly undressed for bed and turned out the lights without even thinking about bracing the chair against her door.

Footsteps woke her and she sat up in the darkness. The footsteps were heavy and measured and they were coming towards her room. She gave a small gasp of fear, remembering too late that she hadn't taken care of the door in her usual fashion. But there had been no need! This was insane! There was no longer any danger in the old house to guard against!

Her thoughts were brought to a jolting end by the door being thrown open. Standing in the dim light of the hallway was Anthony Collins. He had a weird, fixed smile on his lined face and he was holding something at elbow level in his right hand.

"You!" she cried.

"Yes," he said, too pleasantly. His voice was remote, abnormal in a way that brought new panic to her. It was a madman's voice and she thought of those pale blue eyes which had so often made her nervous.

"What do you want?" she asked, holding the bedclothes tightly to her.

"You weren't expecting me," he said in the same odd voice. "Neither were any of the others."

"The others?"

"The maid, Bessie, poor Harriet and my old friend Martin. They were all just as surprised as you when I came to them with the scarab."

"What scarab?" .

"The golden scarab of Rehotip. The golden beetle with its precious stones. Worth a fortune! And I managed to get it and its mate out of Egypt without the authorities any the wiser. I shall always keep them!"

"You're mad!" she whispered.

He came into the room and to her bedside. "Perhaps so," he said, still holding his right hand poised. And now she saw what was in it—one of the giant golden scarabs which she'd seen on his desk and which he had claimed were clever imitations. But this had not been true. They were the genuine thing he'd somehow smuggled out of Egypt without anyone knowing.

"You saw the scarabs and so you must die, just like the others. They all knew I possessed these lovely golden masterpieces. And so I had to kill them."

"No!" she said in horror.

"Not that I wanted to, for I'm a very mild man," he went on in that strange remote voice. "But you'll die very quickly like the others. Just a touch of the poisoned prongs of the scarab and it will be all over. The Egyptians had a fine touch in designing such things. To them it seemed right to combine beauty with a deadly weapon. And the prongs will leave those interesting marks on your throat just as they did with the others."

"The marks!" she gasped. "You made the marks you blamed Barnabas for when you killed those three!"

"And now you are the fourth to die. Best of all, I'm going to make sure the guilt for your death will be thrown on Barnabas. With the marks on your throat it will be easy. So I'll settle two scores at once."

"You mustn't!" she begged, drawing back in the bed. His reply was to lunge at her throat with the pronged golden scarab. And frozen with terror as she was, he might have found his mark if he hadn't suddenly been gripped from behind by strong hands. Barnabas had emerged from the shadowed corner of her room to pounce on the unsuspecting madman.

It was all a nightmare after that. The poisoned scarab fell to the floor and was trampled in the scuffle. At the sight of this, Anthony Collins gave up his struggle. Staring at the ruined masterpiece, he began to sob brokenly.

Barnabas had the unhappy duty of again calling the police in the middle of the night. It was nearly dawn when a police car took Anthony Collins away for treatment in the state asylum. Later, if he recovered sufficiently, he would undoubtedly have to face a trial.

Barnabas stood in the doorway of the red brick house with an arm around Maggie as they watched the red taillights of the police car vanish in the near-dawn.

"How did you know?" she asked, looking up at him.

The gaunt face showed a bitter smile. "He changed his attitude too quickly. I was sure he wasn't that reasonable. For some time I've suspected him of madness."

"Wait until Roger hears about this."

Barnabas nodded. "I fear that cousin Roger is singularly limited in his imagination."

"Thank goodness you aren't, or I'd be dead at this minute." She snuggled close to him.

He seemed uneasy. "I must get back to the old house quickly," he said, "before dawn really arrives. Hare will wonder what happened to me."

"Let me drive you," she said.

Barnabas smiled. "I think that will be safe enough now."

As she started the motor of the station wagon, Maggie said suddenly, "I feel sorry about Quentin. I mean, here he went to all that trouble of pretending to be Herb Price and all, just so he could come back to Collinwood. And look what he got into! I wonder where he is now?"

"Quentin can take care of himself." As he spoke, Barnabas glanced up at the lightening sky. Dawn would break soon.

Obedient to the tension she sensed in him, Maggie pressed the accelerator a bit more firmly. When she halted the car before the door of the old house he leaned over and gave her a brief kiss on the lips.

"A safe journey back," he said, and opened the door on his side in preparation to get out.

"I hate to have you leave me now," she said. "Couldn't you have me in for early coffee? I'm sure Hare wouldn't mind."

Barnabas smiled oddly. "Don't be too certain of that. He's a very gruff, strange fellow. I'll see you later."

"Tonight at Collinwood?"

The gaunt face lost its smile and he looked wistful.

"I'd rather say, one night at Collinwood," he told her. "You know how it is with me. I rarely make definite plans."

"I'll be waiting," she said gently.

"And I will come." He quickly got out of the station wagon and hurried to the steps of the old house. He turned just once to wave goodbye. Then he went inside.

She turned the car around and started back to the red brick house in the growing light of another gray day. A feeling of deep sadness overwhelmed her. It was dawn. And Barnabas had gone from her.